I NOT DAVID

Finding Me Book One

Kameo Monson

I NOT David

For more information about this title or other fictional works by Kameo Monson, please contact her directly at: kmonson.author@gmail.com or visit her website at KameoMonson.com

Cover Design by Wynter Designs
Editing by Craig D. Barton

e-book ISBN: 978-1-7325802-3-7
Print ISBN-13: 978-1-7325802-2-0

FREE DOWNLOAD

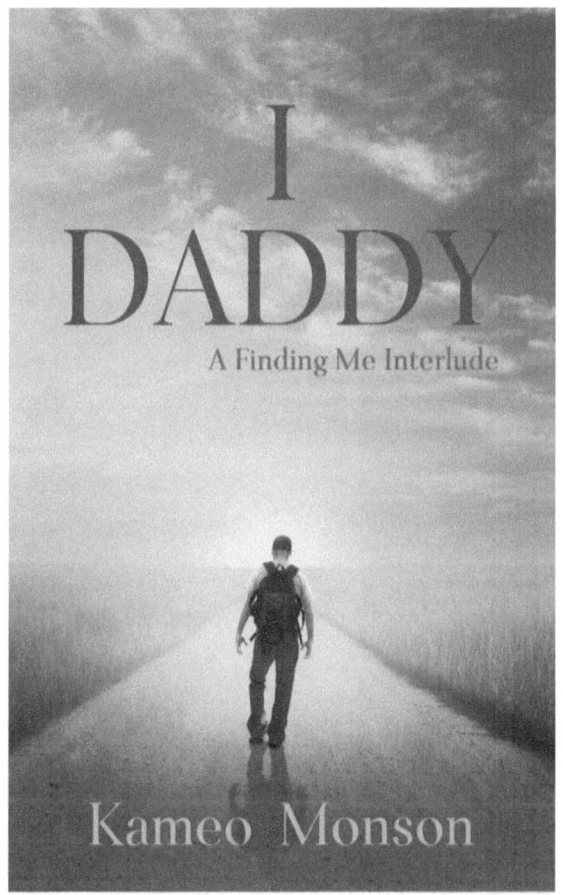

What happens to Derek?
Find out in the full-length novel
I Daddy: A Finding Me Interlude

Download for free at KameoMonson.com

For my son.

Derek's Denial

Kat curled her fingers around the straps of her worn leather purse and glanced at her husband. A comforting smile crossed his face as he took one of her hands in his. Joey lined up blocks on the play table behind them. And seconds ticked by loudly on the clock that hung above the filing cabinet. Kat counted them in rounds of four—a habit leftover from her time as a drum major in high school.

The doctor had left the room to consult with a colleague, promising to be back within a few minutes. It had been ten.

Joey's never-ending tantrums, love of rocking, and leading her around the house by the finger exhausted Kat, but others assured her his behaviors meant nothing. *They're normal,* they would say, smiling as they held their perfectly behaved children. When Joey pulled out every piece of silverware they owned and

1

lined them up on the floor, it seemed cute. Then she'd read an article on autism.

Derek hated the idea of taking Joey to a doctor, but Kat had persisted.

"Are you ready for this?" Kat asked her husband.

He shrugged. "Sure, it's not like there's anything wrong."

She sighed. Why couldn't he see it? The tantrums alone should concern him.

A faint knock sounded on the door, and Dr. Werther stepped into the room and behind his executive desk, then shuffled some papers before sitting down. "Well, we've narrowed it down, and I have some results for you today."

Kat's breathing quickened, and she nodded for him to continue.

"We've run several tests, observed Joey, and interacted with him enough to feel comfortable diagnosing him with autism."

Kat's heart leaped in her chest, landing in her throat.

"What proof do you have of that?" Derek asked.

Dr. Werther narrowed his eyes as he met Derek's gaze. He obviously understood that Derek might require some convincing. "Both of the questionnaires you and your wife filled out point in that direction. We also observed several of the necessary behaviors to make such a diagnosis."

"Like what?" Derek leaned back in his chair and folded his arms over his chest.

Dr. Werther smiled patiently. "Joey lacks typical eye contact, lines up objects for purposes other than play, and struggles with certain tactile experiences such as fabrics, shoes, and food. His speech is slightly impaired, and he has a pragmatics delay."

"Pragmatics?"

"Yes. Pragmatics is the give and take in communication. Not only is it speaking back and forth like we are, but it deals with recognizing the meaning of words based on context. Joey takes things literally."

"He's three," Derek said flatly.

Dr. Werther knit his fingers together as he leaned forward on his desk. "As time goes on, the pragmatics delay may become more prevalent. Therapy now will help him communicate better as he gets older."

Derek rolled his eyes. "We cannot afford therapy."

Kat breathed deeply at the muttered response. She placed her hand on her husband's arm and turned to the doctor. "I read most therapies are offered through the state?"

"They are. You'll have to call the Department of Developmental Disabilities and set up an intake."

A what? Kat watched as Dr. Werther jotted down a number.

"Call here. Tell them Joey has autism and that you need to schedule an intake."

"Okay. What's an intake?"

"The state will send someone out to help you get services started. Joey needs speech and occupational therapy. He may also benefit from ABA—if you can find anyone."

Words. That's all Kat heard. Words that made absolutely no sense. What was occupational therapy? ABA?

"You can also find help through various resources: Autism Speaks, the Autism Society. Look online. There's plenty of information out there."

Derek's chair squeaked on the tile as he stood up. Joey screamed from the table behind them and covered his ears. Was that part of autism?

Dr. Werther held out his hand to Derek, who shook it while staring at the floor. When Kat took the proffered hand, the doctor placed his other hand on top of hers. "Your life will change, but your love for your son won't."

A burning sensation swept across Kat's eyes, and Derek rubbed his hand down her back. He'd take care of her.

"Thank you," she whispered as she gathered Joey in her arms and handed him to Derek to carry.

As they got settled in the car, Kat's rapid heartbeats and breathing refused to calm down. Her hands twisted around her seatbelt, which seemed to tighten with every passing minute. Tears tumbled down her face as thoughts of the future pummeled her mind.

"Derek?" She glanced at her husband, trying to copy his calm demeanor.

"Yeah?"

"How do you feel about all this?"

Derek's right shoulder lifted and fell again. "How am I supposed to feel? I think he's normal, but apparently, I'm wrong."

Kat sniffed, willing words that mirrored her emotions to form. "I know he's the same kid, but what does this mean for him? Will he be able to attend college? What about getting married?"

"I think he's just a little bit autistic. He'll get over it."

All the articles Kat had read said no one got over autism. They improved with therapies. "I don't think that's how it works. It's a spectrum, but I don't think there is a little autistic or a lot autistic. There's just autistic."

Derek sat in silence, and Kat continued staring at him as he pushed a hand through his dark hair.

When he didn't respond, she looked down at her hands and counted to ten. They shook. Twisting to look at their only child, who had fallen asleep in his car seat, she gazed at his chubby cheeks, still red from crying, and his long lashes that matched his fine brown hair. Perfect.

Her face crumpled. "This is stupid. He's my kid. I love him. I don't know what any of these therapies are that the doctor said he needs. I don't understand half of what he said."

Derek patted her knee. "We'll figure it out."

"Will we?"

"Sounds like we don't have much of a choice."

"How are you so calm?" Kat asked.

"I don't know. I still think he'll get over it. He'll be fine."

Kat sighed. "Derek, everything I've read says there's no getting over it."

"We'll see."

Denial. Derek was in denial, and she had no idea how to deal with getting Joey help.

Phonecordectomy

The next morning, Kat woke up to a toy playing *Twinkle, Twinkle, Little Star* in her ear. Joey stood next to her, pushing the play button every time the song ended.

"Hi, Joey."

Joey glanced toward her and picked up her hand, pulling.

"Okay, give me a sec. I'll get up. What do you want?"

Kat twisted her legs over the edge of the bed and asked her question a second time. Joey tugged her hand again. She stood up and allowed him to tow her into the kitchen.

"Joey, what do you want? Do you want breakfast?"

Joey didn't answer, but pushed her hand toward the cabinet holding the cups. She reached in and picked up the blue cup he liked. Calmly taking the cup, he threw it to the floor. She tried again with the red one. This time he held it with two hands.

"Red it is," Kat said. "Joey, say, *I want juice.*"

The little boy flung his body onto the laminate tile in a heap, fine hair gathering static as it swept the floor in front of him. He began to cry.

"Say, *juice, please.*" Kat tried again.

The screaming increased.

Reaching into the fridge, Kat grabbed the apple juice and poured a small amount into the red cup. Joey stood up, not a tear in his eye, took the cup from her hands, and threw it to the ground. Then he crumpled to the floor again, wailing. This time he knocked his head repeatedly on the hard surface. Kat frowned at her son, and tears formed in her eyes. How was she supposed to deal with this?

She leaned over, cleaning the juice off the floor, the rag wiping up her tears too.

With the mess taken care of and Joey still screeching while knocking his head on the laminate, Kat slumped against a lower cabinet.

Joey refused sippy cups by the time he was two. He also refused to tell Kat what color cup he wanted, what he wanted to drink, or how much to pour—all of which, evidently, mattered to him. Kat had learned to read most of Joey's cues, but some still escaped her.

The noise of Derek moving toward the kitchen caught her attention, and she quickly got to her feet and brushed at her backside. Joey remained screaming on the floor, but Kat noticed him glance in her direction before knocking his head the next time.

"What's he crying about now?" Derek asked, peering at Joey as he finished buttoning his uniform.

"I don't know. Something to do with the juice I gave him."

"Will therapy stop him from dumping his drinks or throwing his food?"

Kat shook her head and shrugged. "I hope so. I'll start making calls today."

Derek gave her a quick hug and stepped over to Joey. "Hey, buddy, how about a hug before I go?"

He picked Joey up, who looked at the cabinet again.

"What do you want from there?" Derek asked.

Joey wriggled to get down, and then towed Derek to the cabinet. Instead of opening the door and choosing a cup, Derek picked Joey up. Little hands grabbed the blue cup, identical to the red one Kat had given him earlier.

"I showed him that cup. He threw it to the floor."

"Guess he wants it now."

Derek held out the apple juice, and Joey watched him pour some in the blue cup still clasped in his hands. When Derek stopped, Joey's eyes narrowed.

"Just a little more, buddy."

Derek added a few more splashes to the cup, and Joey's eyes stayed relaxed as he lifted the juice to his mouth. Once finished, Joey placed the cup on the counter and looked at Kat. "Joey want toast."

Kat glanced at Derek and sighed, then picked up the bread on the counter.

"You want toast? Squares or triangles?"

"Circles."

"Circles? Okay."

As Kat reached up to grab a mason jar lid to cut circles out of the toast, Derek wrapped his arms around her waist, brushed her shoulder-length auburn hair away from her neck with his chin, and kissed the soft spot under her ear. "See you after work."

Tears ran down her cheeks as she nodded. "Yeah."

Morning quickly evolved to afternoon, and Kat found herself deep in several tantrums—meltdowns— that's what the doctor had called them. The oddest meltdown started when the handset of the toy phone wouldn't reach Joey's ear without picking up the dialer.

He'd struggled with the toy for ten minutes before Kat took it away. Then he cried in front of the closet door where she had stored it for thirty minutes.

Feeling the pressure of never-ending screams echoing in her head, Kat took the toy out of the closet and snipped the rope connecting the handset to the dialer. She was certain to separate herself from Joey in order to perform the phonecordectomy. With no proof that the rope ever existed, she handed the toy to her son. A second later, the handset landed near the couch, and Joey curled into a ball on the floor eight feet away with an excruciating screech.

"Joey, I have to make some phone calls. Please."

Despite her begging, the shrieking never stopped, and Kat had to make those calls. Stepping into the other room, she dialed the number Dr. Werther had jotted down for her the day before. Several deep breaths coated her lungs, and she counted the rings, hoping to calm her trepidation before dealing with her next nerve-racking experience: the unknown.

"Department of Developmental Disabilities, this is Angie."

"Hi. I...my son was diagnosed with autism yesterday, and his doctor said I should call for an intake so he can start therapy."

"How old is your son?"

"Three."

"His name?"

"Joey Burns. I don't really know anything about this process. Can you explain it to me?"

"Address?"

"5898 East Carnation Street."

"I'm going to send out some paperwork for you to fill out as well as a list of documents we'll need copies of. The diagnosis form the doctor gave you, your son's birth certificate, social security card, and proof of residence."

"Okay." Kat scrambled to write down the documents she needed to gather. "Do I mail everything back?"

"A coordinator will come to your house to conduct the intake interview and collect the documents from you."

"Can you tell me about occupational therapy? I don't know what it is." Kat's heart beat erratically, and her knee began bouncing. How was she ever going to learn everything?

"The coordinator can answer those questions. If your son qualifies, they'll help you determine what therapies he needs. Are you available April twentieth at two o'clock?"

"That's fine."

Joey quietly joined Kat as the phone call ended—his frustrations diminished. She picked him up and carried him to the living room where she sank onto the couch.

"What's your name?" Kat asked, resting her forehead against his as he bounced his three-year-old toddler legs on the couch cushion next to her.

He peered sideways, avoiding her eyes.

"Oh," Kat said, "I know your name. Your name is Donald."

"I not Donald," said Joey.

He was getting better at this game.

"You're not? What's your name?" When Joey didn't answer, Kat continued. "Oh, I know your name. It's John."

"I not John." Joey bounced his legs, a smile threatening to appear on his rosy lips.

"You're not? Then what's your name?"

Still no answer.

"Oh, I know, your name is Spencer."

Joey shook his head, but watched Kat, obviously waiting for her to continue the game.

"You're not Spencer? I was sure that was it. Is your name George?"

Joey shook his head again, and the corner of his mouth turned up.

"No. How about David? Is your name David?"

"I not David. I Joey." Joey jumped toward Kat with a grin on his face.

"No. That's not it," Kat said as she tickled him. "You're not Joey. Your name is definitely David."

Joey giggled as he shook his head. "I not David. I Joey."

"Okay, Joey. I sure do love you."

Hugging Joey as tightly as she could, Kat's heart thrummed. She'd worked hard teaching him to share his name. Eventually, he'd answer when people asked. She hoped.

The turning of Derek's key in the door alerted Kat to his return. Meltdowns and phone calls had interrupted her meal planning for the day. She rushed into the kitchen and searched the pantry.

"Hi, honey," she called when the door closed.

Derek walked into the kitchen. "What's for dinner? I'm starved."

Of course he was. Who else managed a restaurant and came home hungry?

Kat scrunched up her nose and gave him a weak smile. "I made a bunch of phone calls and worked on figuring things out for Joey all day and ran out of time to plan dinner. Give me a sec, and I'll put something together."

She felt the burn of Derek's eyes following her as she moved.

"Kat, relax. Let's go hit McDonald's or something."

Kat exhaled and all the crazy of the day floated away. "Thank you." She hugged her husband.

Together, the couple helped Joey into the car. He fought putting on his shoes, and they decided to ignore his bare feet once again.

Their food came quickly, and they immediately sat in the play area of the busy restaurant. Joey hopped out of Derek's arms and hurried over to the slide. A few minutes later, he came back, stared at the fries before pulling a few out and stuffing them into his mouth, only to run away again with a determined look on his face.

Derek watched Joey and then turned to Kat, his brown eyes meeting her blue. "See, he's doing great. This is perfectly normal."

Kat eyed her husband. "It is. But the tantrums, I mean, meltdowns, he had throughout the day weren't."

"How many did he have?"

She ticked them off on her fingers. "Two over the toy phone. Two about juice. I made him put on his shoes to play outside. And one at the TV."

"So, six?"

"Yup. Each one lasted a minimum of twenty minutes." Kat rested her head in the palm of one hand, supporting herself with an elbow on the table. "I'm wiped."

Another family entered the play area, their five children running with whoops and yells toward the toys. Kat flinched. Within seconds, the sound of Joey screaming reached her ears.

Kat's chest tightened and shallow breathing took over as she watched Derek step to the toys, his fists already formed. Joey stretched out on the bottom of the slide, holding the edges and hitting the back of his head on the plastic tube.

"He won't move," a little girl said.

Derek held his hand out to their son, the muscles in his jaw tightening. "Come on, Joey, you have to give them a turn."

Joey shook his head and continued to bang it on the slide. The little girl's complaints grew louder, and Derek knelt next to Joey. "Do you think we should get ice cream after dinner?"

No answer.

The girl's parents called her over and whispered something in her ear. As she continued to complain with tears rolling down her reddened cheeks, Joey screamed louder and clung to the slide as if it were his only comfort. With no end in sight, Derek grabbed Joey, an exacerbating move, and took him back to the table. "Come on, buddy, let's eat some chicken nuggets."

Joey crashed his head into Derek's chin. As fire smoldered in Derek's eyes, Kat gathered their things. Dinner was over.

It felt like hours by the time Kat slipped into the bedroom where Derek hid. The wailing in the car on the way home and the agony of getting Joey to sleep had only punctuated his silence. But nothing surprised her when it ended.

"I'm done taking him out." Derek slammed his toothbrush into its holder. "It doesn't matter what we do, he's always screaming."

"It's because of the noise and the chaos. He was fine until that family showed up." Kat lowered her head, giving her husband a sideways glance from her side of the bed.

"You can take him all you want, but I don't like making scenes." Derek scooted down in the bed, facing Kat. As she started to cry, he opened his arms and pulled her closer.

"He can't help it, Derek. Today I read that kids with autism get overwhelmed by all kinds of things their bodies can't process. Lights. Sounds. According to experts, a change in what they expect can throw them off too."

"He's going to have to learn, Kat. He can't get away with things just because he has autism." Derek fingered the hair at the top of her head.

"I know, but we need to teach him with patience." She curled into his shoulder. "I wish I knew how."

Silence smothered the conversation, and Kat rolled away from Derek when he started to snore. Worry for her family roiled within her, while sleep avoided her beck and call.

Giving up, she climbed out of bed and wandered to the computer where she began searching autism sites. Joey needed help, and she refused to wait for others to teach her how to wade through the process. Besides, the day's phone calls to various resources had been useless. Not one person explained what occupational therapy was or how services worked.

April twentieth took forever to come, until it appeared. Then Kat shook with concern. Was she ready for the intake?

The pages of paper slid across each other with a soft scratching sound as Kat flipped through them to make sure she had everything she needed.

The questions in the pamphlet they'd mailed were ridiculous, requiring her to answer some that obviously had no bearing on her son. Her favorite one inquired if Joey had ever been convicted of a crime. She'd scribbled *he's three.*

Other questions boggled her already confused mind. Joey brought Kat his shoes when he wanted to go somewhere, but if she asked him to get his shoes, he refused every time. Moreover, he knew his name, but getting him to say it? That's why they still played their little game.

The doorbell rang, and Kat brushed her hand across her blouse, smoothing it out. Shaking her hands near her sides first, she opened the door. A pile of folders and books supported by two arms stood in front of her.

"Mrs. Burns?"

"Yes." Kat opened the door wide, but the woman holding the files remained outside.

"I'm Ginger with the Department of Developmental Disabilities—the DDD, we have an appointment."

The woman's voice reminded Kat of the customer service representatives at the Department of Motor Vehicles.

"Yes. Come in. We can sit at the table in the kitchen."

"Thank you."

The two women sat down, and Ginger scanned the room. "Who is the intake for?"

Kat wrung her hands. "My son, Joey."

Ginger scratched his name across a page that appeared similar to the one Kat had filled out earlier. "Have you contacted Long Term Care yet?"

"No. Was I supposed to?"

No one had said anything about Long Term Care.

"Well, they fund the services. So, if your son qualifies with the DDD, he has to qualify with Arizona Long Term Care in order to receive any therapies. I can help you with that process."

"Okay." Another process to learn?

Ginger glimpsed down at the paper in front of her and asked Kat the exact same questions she had answered on the paperwork that had arrived in the mail. What a waste of government spending. She could have sent the thing in for less than a dollar. However, Kat did appreciate the opportunity to have some of the questions explained.

"Can Joey grasp a spoon?"

Kat's brows furrowed. "Do you want to know if he can feed himself?"

"How you answer is up to you. Can he hold a spoon by himself?"

"Yeah, he can hold the spoon in his hand, but he can't feed himself without making a huge mess."

"Can he stand on one foot?"

Kat sighed. "I tried to get him to, but he wouldn't try. I'm not sure."

"Do you think he can?"

Kat raised her brows and shook her head. "I don't know. Maybe."

"Does Joey know how to ride a bicycle?"

"No, but he can ride a tricycle. That's typical for his age."

"Can Joey dress himself?"

"He's capable, but he refuses to do it without my help."

"And where do you see Joey in five years?"

Joey started banging a toy he was frustrated with and stole Kat's attention.

"Joey," Kat said, "bring it here." She looked at Ginger with tears in her eyes then back at Joey. "Let me show you how it works."

Joey brought the toy to Kat, but when she started to show him what the toy did, he grabbed it out of her hand and threw it to the floor. Not a split second passed before his body sprawled across the tile where he banged his head.

"Five years?" She bit her lip and swallowed hard. "Despite these types of behaviors, we see him in a regular classroom and finished with therapy."

Ginger smiled wanly. "Well, maybe. You never know." Looking down at the table, she picked up the forms as she said, "I'll need you to send me copies of his birth certificate, social security card, and proof of residence by next week."

Kat handed Ginger the documents. "I copied them for you earlier." *This is ridiculous.*

"Great. You should receive notification within thirty days letting you know whether or not he qualifies."

Kat rolled her eyes. "Do you have the information on Long Term Care?"

Ginger placed the pile of folders back on the table. "I do. Let me see… call this number and ask for an intake." Ginger handed her a Long Term Care informational card. "If you wait until he's qualified with the DDD, you may have a better chance. They've been rejecting more people recently. You really should apply for Social Security too."

Social Security? "Why?"

"It helps pay for his needs. You can buy clothing and food or pay for schooling."

"Isn't Social Security based off income?"

"It is, but they raised the amount a family can earn recently. You should apply, you never know." Ginger shrugged.

"Thank you. I'll look into that." Kat wasn't applying for Social Security.

"Sure. So, you should hear something within a month."

"Sounds good. Thanks for coming."

Kat closed the door and eased down to the floor. *I can't do this. I'll never learn all this stuff. Long Term Care? What does the DDD do, anyway?*

The Fan

Two months later, Kat stretched her legs out as she sat on the floor. Her stiff tailbone fought the movement, sending stabbing pains through her backside. She cringed. Taking a block from the middle of Joey's line, she placed it on the top of her castle. Screams immediately saturated the air but stopped when Kat knocked down the castle and put the stolen block back in Joey's line. She hoped by building her own castle, she might encourage him to build one too. The process of stealing blocks seemed like a good way to get him used to unexpected events. Of course, he only calmed down when Kat returned the block.

As the light pink in the sky turned purple, Derek walked in the door, a pile of mail filling his arms. Kat tried to stand, but her tailbone revolted and she yelled, "Watch out!"

Too late.

The first few blocks of Joey's line slid across the floor when Derek unknowingly kicked them. Joey screamed, and Kat picked up his flailing body, then followed Derek into the kitchen.

"How was your day?" she asked.

"Okay, I guess. People just kept coming in, and three servers called out sick. I barely got a break."

"Sorry."

"Hey, as long as people eat Baja Burgers, I'll have a job. Look at the bright side, right?"

"Right, Mr. Manager."

Derek pecked Kat on the lips and rubbed the top of Joey's head. "Hey Joey, what's wrong?"

"You kicked a few blocks out of line." Kat moved over to where Derek flipped through the mail. "Did we get anything good? Anything from the state?"

"Not sure. Here's something from ALTC."

Kat grabbed the envelope and handed Joey off to Derek. Ripping it open she shook the single piece of paper. Her bottom lip trembled as she stared at the form before throwing it on the counter.

"He gets nothing. Nothing!"

"I thought you said he qualified."

"He qualified for the DDD, but he has to qualify for Arizona Long Term Care too. I don't understand what happened. They asked all the same stupid questions." She flung both arms in the air. "He needs help, Derek! We can't keep going like this. I can't handle the thousands of meltdowns anymore."

Kat slumped onto the couch where she motioned for Derek to give her Joey. "Love you, Joey."

He wiggled away, still screaming, as she worked to stifle her own tears. Comforting Joey while having her own meltdown accomplished little, but she had to try.

Derek sat next to them and wrapped his arm around Kat and their screaming son. "Maybe you should call someone."

"I'll call the DDD lady tomorrow and see where we go from here." Softening her voice, she asked, "Would you mind helping him fix his line of blocks? We've waited too long, so he'll probably keep screaming, but who knows."

Derek climbed down to the floor with Joey and handed him a block he'd kicked. Joey carefully focused on the block before curling his fingers around it and throwing it a few feet away.

"Joey. We don't throw things. Let's put the blocks away," Derek said.

"I don't know if he understands. Maybe if we all try to play together he'll do better."

"We need to teach him the way we would teach any other kid. If he throws a block, they get put away."

Kat climbed down to the floor and pulled Joey onto her lap. "Come on, Joey, let's play with the blocks, okay?"

She started to build a tower. As Derek huffed and placed a block at the end of the line, Joey climbed off Kat's lap and ran to pick up the block he'd thrown to help his dad.

As soon as the DDD opened the next morning, Kat called and spoke with Ginger. When that call ended, she hurried to dial ALTC, only to find herself anxiously awaiting their return call. But as the day wore on and hope diminished, she gave into Joey's desire to play the Bricks app on her phone. What agency returned calls late in the day?

The ringing startled Joey, and the phone fell to the floor before Kat caught it. She handed him a toy and sprinted to her room, locking the door before the final ring.

"Hello."

"Hello. This is Sue with Arizona Long Term Care. I am returning a call from Kathryn Burns."

Kat's shoulders relaxed as her heart rate increased. "Yes, this is Kat. I called in reference to my son, Joey."

"Birth date?"

Kat rattled off the necessary information so Sue could find Joey in the system. As she waited, she breathed in, then slowly exhaled. Her racing heart refused to calm down, but she did find it easier to speak.

"What can I help you with today, Mrs. Burns?" Sue asked.

Kat waited to answer until the clicks on the distant keyboard stopped.

"My son was denied Long Term Care, and I would like to appeal the decision."

After searching several websites, she had her battle plan. Setup another intake and deny any skills he hadn't completely mastered. Following the advice was her last chance for a year.

More clicking sounded. "Just a moment while I check...Oh...it looks like we don't have an opening for another sixty days."

Kat's heart thudded wildly in her chest again, and she groaned. "Do you have a cancellations list?"

"I do, but that's too long. I'm going to place you on hold and see what I can do. One moment."

Tears clouded Kat's vision. She tried not to focus on the screaming that now resonated from the other side of the closed door. If she called to him, it would only get worse. Her fist found its way to her mouth, and she bit down on the fatty portion of her index finger. A shuffling sound alerted her to Sue's return.

"Mrs. Burns?"

"Yes." Kat exhaled slowly, trying to ease the discomfort in her chest.

"Looking through the notes from your intake, I see that you were not certain about several answers. I'm going to ask you a few questions now and see if we can rectify this situation over the phone."

A sudden intake of air lit through Kat's lungs. "Thank you. I appreciate it."

"Of course. Would you say Joey can feed himself?"

"No."

"Can he grasp a spoon?"

"He can hold the spoon, but he cannot use it appropriately."

"Can Joey use the bathroom by himself?"

"No. He's still in diapers." *He's three. Aren't diapers still normal?*

"Can Joey dress himself?"

25

"No." Kat chose not to expound on her answer this time.

"Tell me about some of Joey's other behaviors."

She closed her eyes and tried to stop the tears from flowing past the edges of her eyes, but failed.

"He has four or five, sometimes six meltdowns a day. Each one lasts a minimum of twenty minutes. A lot of the time they are twice that."

"What causes the meltdowns?"

"What doesn't?" She sighed. "How his drink is poured. Or when he decides I've given him the wrong cup, he'll throw it to the floor with his body and bang his head on the tile. He'll only wear knit clothing. He breaks down when we get stuck in a crowd or when we're grocery shopping. Wearing shoes. Half of the time, I don't know why he's upset, just that he is. Food is a problem too."

"Is he in any kind of preschool?"

Kat's lip trembled, and her voice squeaked. "I'm waiting to hear back from the school district to schedule his testing. The other preschool we tried asked him to leave."

The clacking of computer keys filled the next few seconds, finally slowing into silence.

"A case manager will reexamine Joey's file. You can expect to hear from us within thirty days. If he qualifies for Long Term Care, he'll receive full medical and dental, and any therapies approved by the DDD will be covered."

"Thank you. Can you tell me whether or not you think he'll qualify?"

"I'm sorry, I can't."

Kat nodded at no one in particular as the silence in the hallway registered in her mind. Joey had stopped screaming.

"I understand. Thank you."

Hanging up, she opened the bedroom door. Joey's legs curled under his belly as he slept, his reddened face, nearly hidden within his arms, stained by salty tears. Aware that the late nap meant a restless night for the house, she covered him with a light blanket. Sometimes choosing solace in the present required forsaking solace in the future. At least that's what she told herself.

Three weeks later, a nervous current ran through Kat's arms when she opened another letter from ALTC. She'd already cleaned up several spilled drinks that day, causing her sanity to beg for help. This could be it. As the glue on the envelope separated, she wondered what she would do if he was denied again. What could she do? The paper slipped out with reverence, as if the words would change if not given proper respect. *Please, let him be approved.*

She closed her eyes as she unfolded the paper. After a deep breath, she peered down at the letter, her eyes immediately falling to the words *you are eligible.* She smiled even as her heart beat harder in her chest. The bottom of the page included a temporary ID card.

Following the instructions, she immediately called Joey's DDD case manager.

Having heard the hum of Derek's car in the driveway toward the end of the call, Kat ran out to greet him. She hopped from one foot to another, both from excitement and from the hot concrete. Derek smiled at her as he shut the car door. "This is an unexpected greeting."

"How was your day?" Kat leaned in for a quick welcome-home peck.

"Pretty good. I received a little gift from Steve today."

"You did? What for?"

"Don't sound so surprised." Derek chuckled.

Kat shook her head. "Sorry. I meant to ask if the gift was for something specific. What did you get?"

The heat from the concrete seeped deeper into Kat's feet, and she hurried inside, Derek a single step behind.

Joey crouched next to an outlet with a five-inch desktop fan, plugging and unplugging it from the wall.

"What's he doing?"

The question confused Kat until she remembered she hadn't mentioned the fan to Derek. "He learned how to take out the protective covers and kept trying to put things in the outlets. I couldn't stop him, so I gave him a fan and worked with him until he learned not to touch the prongs. It's safer this way."

"How is that safer? He's going to electrocute himself. Stop giving in to his behaviors."

"What am I supposed to do? There are times he has to be by himself, like when I shower, unless you prefer me dirty."

Derek's demeanor darkened. "That's not what I'm saying. He needs to learn to never touch an outlet."

"Okay, you tell me how to teach him that quickly. Because I spent several hours today chasing him around the house to keep him away from outlets."

Derek took the fan from Joey, who burst into tears and began hitting his head on the wall.

"Joey, stop screaming," he said, pursing his lips.

Kat walked toward the kitchen. "That won't work. He doesn't stop crying just because you tell him to."

"He needs discipline."

She turned around and glared at her husband. "All kids do, but no three-year-old responds when they are told to stop screaming."

Joey screamed louder. Kat rushed over and picked him up.

"Give me the fan. I want to show you something." She raised her eyes to meet Derek's angry glare.

He handed her the fan, and Joey quieted as he placed his hand on the base.

Kat held the end of the cord out to Joey. "Joey, where can you touch?"

He studied the cord carefully, then took the thick plastic surrounding the prongs in his hand.

"Do you touch here?" She pointed, but didn't touch the prongs.

Joey shook his head. "Ouch."

"That's right, ouch."

She gently took the plug from his hands and held it prongs-first toward him, moving it forward slowly. Joey shifted so the prongs couldn't touch him.

"He won't touch the prongs. He won't even let me touch him with the prongs. This is safer than letting him find toys and forks to shove in an outlet when I'm

29

in the bathroom or locked in the bedroom because I have to get away from the screaming. You're at work all day. I'm here dealing with meltdowns, spills, and missing outlet covers."

Derek snatched the fan out of Joey's hands again.

As Joey shrieked, Kat closed her eyes and breathed deeply, hoping the tears would subside before spilling onto her cheeks.

"Can you keep him quiet, please?" he hissed through his teeth.

Derek traipsed toward the kitchen, clenching his fists tighter. Once the fan rested on top of the fridge where Joey couldn't reach, he sighed.

Kat sat on the floor with their son, trying to redirect his attention. The screaming continued.

"He qualifies for Long Term Care now. We got the letter today. I've got a list of companies to call to start setting up therapies."

Derek nodded.

"What gift did you receive?" Her voice was calmer than it had been, but remained tight.

"What?"

She shook her head, giving up. Shouting over Joey's wailing never worked.

Thirty minutes later, Joey rocked himself in the rocking chair. Kat had put him there after twenty minutes of lining up blocks, watching TV, and holding him on her lap. It appeared the chair was the answer.

Derek had disappeared into another room when their conversation—fight—had ended, and Kat wondered whether to track him down or let him stew some more. She pulled out some pot pies, slipped them into the oven, and went in search of her husband.

Derek sat on the bed and glared at his tablet's screen, refusing to look up when she walked into the bedroom. "Are you sure you can leave him alone without his fan?"

"He's in his chair. I can hear it squeaking." Her words held a bite to them that she longed for him to ignore. "Dinner will be ready in a few."

He nodded.

Kat climbed on the bed next to him. "Derek?"

He eyed her from the side before returning his gaze to the tablet.

"I won't give him the fan. I can tell that's important to you. I just get so frustrated. It's hard being the one with him all day long without a break."

"I don't get a break either."

The words stung. Any kind of work without constant crying seemed like a vacation to her.

"I know. And I know you deal with customers and employees and deliveries at work. I can't imagine doing that and then coming home to a tired wife and Joey's constant meltdowns."

"It's not that bad. But we need to find a way to teach him how to act appropriately." He wrapped his arm around Kat, pulling her against him.

Her lips thinned, and she exhaled slowly through her nose. "Yeah. Therapy should help."

He nodded again.

"Derek?"

"Hmm?"

"What gift did you get today? I tried to ask earlier, but you couldn't hear me over the crying."

He turned to face her, a smile spreading across his lips. "Steve gave us tickets to a D-backs game on Saturday."

"Oh...for us or for Joey too?"

"Three tickets."

"Great." Kat pushed her fist against her left leg, to keep it still. The idea of Joey at a baseball game terrified her, but she didn't have the energy for that discussion. "Dinner should be ready. Come on out."

Diamondbacks Dilemma

Friday night, Kat curled into Derek's shoulder as they lay in bed and traced a random pattern on his chest. His hand slid further down her back. It was time.

"When is the game tomorrow?"

"Five."

She paused and gathered her thoughts before responding. "I'm worried about taking Joey. He doesn't do well with noise."

"He'll be fine."

Kat rubbed his chest some more, knowing it helped keep him calm. "What if he isn't? What if he melts down?"

"He won't." Derek sighed. "You don't want to go?"

"I do. I just... you get embarrassed by his meltdowns, and I don't want—"

Derek moved his hand back to her shoulders. "He'll be fine, but we can always leave if we need to."

"Wouldn't you like to stay? You haven't been to a game in a long time."

"Staying would be nice, but if we need to leave..." He shrugged.

"You'd be okay with that?"

"He needs to learn how to be around noise. But if he's throwing a fit, then we'll leave. No big deal."

Kat wasn't sure how much Derek meant what he said. He plainly wanted them to go as a family, but she had yet to see him handle a public meltdown without some sort of embarrassment. His reactions regularly caused her own anxieties to flare. A three-year-old meltdown was nothing compared to a thirty-four-year-old's.

The next afternoon, Kat gathered a few items to take to the game for Joey. A bag of Goldfish; a peanut-butter-only sandwich, cut in a circle shape; and a few small toys. A couple extra diapers and wipes were also added to her bag. She couldn't wait for the day Joey showed interest in potty training.

As she shouldered the bag, Derek whisked Joey into the living room, flying him through the air like an airplane. The boy giggled when a slight breeze whipped through his hair before he landed on the couch.

"Okay, buddy, let's put your shoes on."

Joey shook his head and squirmed away from the shoe Derek held in his hand.

"Joey, do you want to go to a baseball game?" Derek asked in a sing-song voice.

His son stared at him blankly, rolled his body to the floor, and took off running. Quick to his feet, Derek chased him down, then tickled him to the carpet.

"We're going to a baseball game, and you have to wear your shoes. Come on, once they're on, you can fly around the room again."

Joey wiggled and kicked his foot until Derek caught it. As he attempted to put the shoe on his son's foot, the boy rolled to his belly, changing the position of his foot, then banged his head on the rug.

Kat watched from a few feet away. "It's easier to put them on in the car."

"It's fine." Derek huffed.

He tightened his grip on Joey's ankle and pushed the shoe on over the sock. Joey screamed and yanked his foot away, then held it in his hands.

"Did you hurt him?" She'd barely stopped herself from lunging toward Joey. "He doesn't usually grab his foot like that."

"No. He's angry." Derek forced the other shoe on and trod his way into the kitchen for a handful of Goldfish from the box. "'bout ready?"

"Yeah. Let's go." Kat smiled at her husband, wanting this family activity to work out. Suddenly, two small feet came into view as Joey ran up to her barefoot—his shoes and socks strewn across the living room. She closed her eyes and pinched the top of her nose.

"Joey, where are your shoes?" she asked.

Joey's eyebrows creased, hooding his darkened eyes.

"Get your shoes, Joey." A streak of anger colored Derek's voice.

"No shoes." Joey ran to the living room, picked up a shoe and flung it as hard as he could to the floor.

Derek grabbed his son, spanked the back of his leg, and dropped him unceremoniously onto the couch.

"Derek. Stop."

He glared at Kat, mirroring the look Joey had given her only seconds before.

She let out an exasperated sigh as her head moved left and then right. "Grab him and his shoes. I'll put them on once he's in his seat."

"Why bother? He'll just take them off again."

"Then I'll wait until we get there. Come on."

Derek picked up Joey. "Come on, bud, let's get in the car."

Kat groaned. How on earth would they get through a baseball game if these two couldn't get through packing up to leave?

The uneventful drive downtown helped calm Kat's nerves. And soon, Derek turned into a five-dollar lot, then followed the attendant's directions to the empty spot.

Kat peeked back at the docile toddler. "Joey, I have something to show you, but you need to wear your shoes, okay?"

Joey looked down at the tablet screen in front of him, still watching the cartoon Derek had set up before leaving. She reached back and paused it.

"Joey," she said firmly, getting his attention. "If you let me put your shoes on, you can have a motorcycle."

She showed him the toy motorcycle she'd brought, and he reached for it. Climbing out of the car and opening his door, she leaned inside, picked up a sock, and moved toward his foot. The foot disappeared further into his seat.

"Joey, do you want the motorcycle? Give me your foot."

She gently tugged his foot forward until she could put his sock on.

Every time Joey rejected her action, she reminded him that he could play with the motorcycle as soon as his shoes were on. The process took several minutes, and Derek paced behind the car. "Hurry, we'll miss the national anthem."

Kat rolled her eyes. "Give me a minute."

"You've had five." Derek flashed a half smile.

"Yep, and I might need five more," she said as she set Joey on the ground.

He ran into Derek's arms, who swung him around and back to the ground. "Ready for a walk?"

Derek took his son's hand in his and gave Kat another smile.

She followed behind as Joey took three steps to every one of her husband's. How could she not grin?

The closer the small family got to the stadium, the more people crowded around them. Joey continued to curve his body closer to Derek's, but Derek didn't seem to notice. With a couple extra shuffling steps, Kat sidled up next to her husband and suggested he carry their son, whose muscles had tensed several times since leaving the car.

Rounding the corner to the entrance, a whimper escaped her lips. The throng of noisy people stood together in a haphazard line, waiting to enter the stadium.

Breathe.

She protected Joey from the pandemonium with her body as Derek held him in his arms. Every time the boy squirmed, she pointed at the toy motorcycle in his hand or spun the wheel. For the moment, it was enough.

"Bag please."

Kat handed the attendant her purse.

As it was searched, Joey spotted the bag of Goldfish and wriggled in his father's arms. Soon, he found himself on Derek's shoulders, where wriggling was harder. When Kat slung the bag over her shoulder again, he leaned to the side, trying to get into it.

"Just a minute, Joey. We have to get to our seats," Kat said.

They stepped through the doors and were immediately thrown into the chaotic sway. Some people stood grouped together, while others tried to cross the oncoming foot traffic from both directions. Disjointed as it seemed, lines flowed similarly to the bedlam of rush hour.

Still, it took no time at all for a large man to ram into Kat from behind as he forced his way into the crowd.

"You okay?" Derek asked when she stopped to assess the situation.

"Yeah."

"We should be right over here."

After crossing to the section threshold, Derek led them through the crowd and up some stairs. Without notice, Joey flung his body against Derek's head and screamed. He soon found himself in his father's arms instead of on his shoulders.

Kat winced. "He dropped his toy."

One foot perched on the next stair, she searched what she could see with no success. *Why are we here?* She closed her eyes and applied pressure to her forehead with two fingers and a thumb as she exhaled. Derek clung to Joey, keeping him from wiggling out of his arms.

"Take him to the seats. I'll go look for it," Kat said, then mumbled to herself, "It'll be a miracle if I find it."

Her eyes swept the floor, making sure to reach the corners of every stair as she retraced her steps. Feet moving in the opposite direction slid out of her way. This time, she pushed through the crowd. But she didn't bump into anyone.

Halfway behind a trash can, near the bottom of the stairs, shone a small, green piece of plastic. Kat grabbed at the toy. The handlebars fell off. She cursed. *Broke the same way they always do.*

She pushed the handlebars back into place, where they would stay for a bit. But it wouldn't take long for Joey to realize it was broken. Usually, she kept a new motorcycle with her for this reason alone, but she hadn't had time to buy a spare since the last time one broke.

The organ started playing. The crowd cheered. She had to get back to Joey. Now he'd be screaming over the noise as much as the toy. Sprinting up the stairs, her eyes searched for Derek. A mangled cry alerted her to where her family had settled. Passing six people on the right, she finally sat in the seat next to Derek, who held Joey facing away from him on his lap. Joey spotted the motorcycle in Kat's hand and stopped mid-wail. Grabbing the toy, he spun the front wheel, and the handlebars fell off. The rest of the motorcycle soon flew through the air, Kat unable to catch it. Joey's body tensed, and he flailed his head into Derek's chin before turning to jelly and sliding to the ground.

With Joey crumpled at Derek's feet, Kat picked up her purse, remembering the way Joey had spotted the Goldfish while in line. As her fingers wrapped around the bag, she offered him three of the fish-shaped crackers. The screaming stopped, and he stuffed them into his mouth. She gently convinced him to sit on her lap and handed him three more crackers, waiting to stand for *The Star Spangled Banner*.

When the national anthem ended, Kat sat down, pulled Joey back to her lap, and quickly covered his ears with her palms. Cheering fans waved and shouted for their favorite players. Some whooped and whistled. Kat prayed. Joey ate Goldfish.

The first few innings passed quickly. Only a few players hit the ball, and only one had scored. Each time the audience cheered, Kat covered her son's ears. The commentator was often the loudest, but his voice didn't seem to bother Joey too much.

Eventually, he pushed off her knees and stood next to Derek. Kat watched as her husband picked him up and talked about the game while pointing at the field. Joey's hands slid into Derek's, who helped him clap. Joey grinned. Comforting warmth blanketed Kat's chest as she watched. Derek had been right.

The seventh-inning stretch brought more crowds moving in every direction. They knew better than to move. Staying put, they watched the five minutes of fun down on the field.

"Kat, he's poopy."

Derek stood up and waited for a diaper and wipes.

She raised an eyebrow at him. "I can take him. Are there changing tables for you to use?"

"I saw a family bathroom back there. We'll be fine."

She handed him the bag of supplies and watched them leave. What a miracle.

Not much later, her phone vibrated in her pocket.

Derek: *Come now. Turn left. We're by the bathroom.*

She texted back: *What happened?*

She received no response. Rushing down the stairs and out to the left, she searched for the bathrooms. Finally, she saw Derek standing by the wall under a men's room sign, holding Joey, who wore nothing but a diaper.

"What happened?" she asked when she reached them.

"I got him in there and laid him down, and he started sticking his finger in the poop."

"Where are his clothes?"

"In the trash." Anger laced his voice.

"Why?"

"We're leaving."

Kat swallowed deeply. "Okay."

She followed Derek who bolted out of the stadium. His fast pace kept her from voicing the questions running through her head. Once outside, she stopped. "Please slow down."

Derek turned and gaped at her.

"What happened to his clothes?" she asked as she took a step, indicating they could go on.

"He wiped big gobs of poop all over them. I wasn't going to carry them around." He glowered at her from the side, and she knew not to respond.

Halfway to the car, Kat heard Derek mumbling. "Why do I try to do these kinds of things?" He turned to Kat. "Shouldn't he be potty-trained by now? Can't you at least teach him to keep his hands off his ass?"

She raised an eyebrow. He was angry at her? "You tell me how, and I will. Plenty of kids aren't potty-trained at his age."

"Do they play with their turds? He was freaking Picasso in there."

Kat clenched her jaw, willing herself to stay quiet as she snatched Joey from Derek's arms and continued walking to the car.

"There were people in there, Kat."

She stopped and gaped at him with wide eyes. "You didn't go to the family bathroom?"

"I tried but it was locked with no one in there."

"You took him into the men's room? Was there a changing table?"

"Yeah. And everyone watched him paint the walls. Then I had to clean it up."

Kat pursed her lips as she nodded. "I'm really sorry."

She rubbed her hand down his arm, but he jerked it away.

"He starts therapy next week. I'll talk with the therapists and see if they can help," she said flatly.

With a bounce, she heaved Joey higher onto her hip and walked toward the car. Derek huffed beside her, his eyes filled with disgust—all happiness from earlier forgotten.

At the car, Kat removed the towel she'd placed over Joey's car seat. He struggled and yanked at the towel as she placed it on his chest. The buckles were hot, despite the sun having gone down.

"Joey, please. I don't want you to get burned."

He arched his back and shook his head as he grabbed at the towel again. A single tear escaped Kat's eye as she forced his body down into the seat and buckled the latches, then adjusted the straps.

"Joey, leave the towel there."

He shook his head again and screamed. She glanced at Derek. His narrowed eyes and clenched jaw frightened her more than Joey's crying.

She never questioned their safety, but she hated the anger. It lasted so long, and she worried about the relationship her husband had with their son. After all, hadn't the experts said relationships between parent and child are forged when they are young? Well, Derek liked Joey as long as Joey did what Derek wanted. How does anyone teach a three-year-old to act like a ten-year-old? How could she teach her husband to handle their son's behaviors without becoming embarrassed?

"Joey, stop that screaming! You couldn't handle the game, and we left. Now stop!" Derek slammed his hand down on the steering wheel, clenching his jaw tighter.

Kat glanced back at Joey. The towel had slipped below the chest guard, and the hot plastic rested on his skin. Reaching back, her fingertips brushed the guard. It had cooled down enough not to burn him, but the discomfort of the rough edges across his skin had likely added to his mood.

"The buckle's bothering him."

"That's his fault. He should have kept his hand where it belonged."

"He's three, Derek. I'm sorry he embarrassed you."

Kat closed her eyes and counted.

"Yeah, he embarrassed me. People were staring at us!"

She sighed. "I know. But he can't help it, and we choose whether or not to feel embarrassed."

"Whatever. I'm done taking him places anyway, so it won't matter."

Bolting Barefoot

Kat found herself awake before anyone else the next morning. Joey had slept through the night, leaving her with the ability to get some of the extra rest she needed. A pile of blocks lay strewn across the living room floor, a few left in a line. She stepped over them and ambled to the kitchen where she poured herself a glass of juice. A light breeze tickled her cheek and almost seemed to cool the warming air as she went outside.

Shaded from the morning sun, the small patio held a folding chair, and a few wind chimes. The green grass and a few scattered wildflowers she and Joey had planted were the only pieces of nature she owned.

It was an unusual morning. Most of the time, she sweltered in July—even the early hours were hot. Still, for now, she enjoyed the little bit of solace available to her.

As she sat down, memories of the night before pounded at her head, but she tried to silence them, pushing them into the deepest depths of her mind. She yearned for silence. The kind of silence that stole ruminations, leaving her mind blank. Those moments were rare.

A hummingbird flew into the yard, and she watched as it fluttered near one of the taller wildflowers. A smile crossed her face as she remembered planting them.

Wildflower seeds weren't planted so much as sown. It reminded her of feeding chickens, though she had no idea how to do that.

She'd purchased a few packets of wildflower seeds and surprised Joey with them earlier in the year. The intention was to sprinkle the seeds along the edge of the fence. Joey had decided he liked throwing them into the air above his head. He'd giggled every time they peppered his hair before landing on the ground. Most of the flowers grew along the edge of the yard, but a few made it several feet into the lawn. Derek always mowed around those flowers, leaving them especially for her.

She sighed. What could she do to help Derek and Joey? Those two boys were her life. She wanted nothing more than to hold them both in her arms and hug them forever. Derek loved Joey. She knew that. But he let so much get to him, so much bother him, that she worried he might eventually give up.

He couldn't. Parents don't give up on their children. Not really. Not the good ones. The therapists started tomorrow. Kat could learn to communicate with Joey, to help him understand the world. Change would come. Everything would be okay. That's what she told herself.

"Kat"—Derek stuck his head out the door—"he's crying."

She looked up at her husband. "Where is he?"

Derek shrugged and walked away from the door, anger still raging within his eyes.

Kat finished her juice, closed her eyes, and took a deep, calming breath before standing to enter the house. After setting her glass in the sink, she moved down the hall to Joey's room. His rocking chair leaned against the wall, refusing to rock. Joey sat in it throwing his body into the back of it, screaming.

"Hey Joey. Looks like your chair's stuck. How about I help you?"

She slid the chair out, and Joey startled slightly as the chair rocked back with his body. Sniffling, he gulped air into his lungs, and the crying stopped.

"Are you hungry?" she ran her fingers through his fine hair. "I can make toast."

He scrambled out of the rocker and ran to the kitchen. Kat followed behind and frowned when Derek ignored them as they passed.

The process of making Joey toast took more time than preparing it for others. First, she had to determine what he wanted on the toast, and then she had to figure out if he wanted it cut. As she went through the motions, she hoped Joey would agree to talk, or at least give short answers.

But with the first pieces of toast thrown to the floor and then the trash, she cut the next slices into eight squares and topped them with peanut butter before joining Derek on the couch.

"You gave into him again." Derek didn't look up from his tablet.

"What?"

"The toast. He shouldn't have gotten more. He needs to eat what you give him the first time."

"He'd never eat if I did that."

Derek glared over the top of his tablet. "He'd learn."

Kat rolled her eyes. She'd really hoped he would be over the whole baseball thing.

"I'm sorry," she said, acerbically.

She sat there for a beat, trying to control her own anger. What made him think she hadn't tried forcing Joey to eat what was served? She had. Several times. The last time, she finally gave in at dinner. What was she supposed to do, let him go an entire day without food? And why hadn't he checked on Joey that morning?

"You know, he was crying this morning because his chair was stuck against the wall and wouldn't rock."

"Hmm."

The acknowledgment was thin—too thin.

"All you had to do was walk in there and pull the chair out for him."

Derek ignored her.

"Look, I know you're angry about last night."

"I'm over it."

Kat gaped at her husband in disbelief.

"No you're not. You haven't said a single nice thing to either of us. You're as angry as you were last night. You just don't want to admit it."

He flicked his finger at the tablet, switching pages.

"Do you have to stare at that thing?"

He clenched his jaw and put the tablet down. "I was reading, and you started getting mad."

Silence filled the heavy space between them as Kat tried to sift her way through the conversation.

"You made that asinine comment about the toast."

"It's true, you shouldn't be remaking his food."

"Fine. You do it your way."

She stood up from the couch, grabbed her purse from the floor, and rushed out the front door.

Key in hand, Kat jerked the car door open and slumped into the driver's seat. Tears rolled down her cheeks, and she brushed them away as horrid wails issued from her lips. She choked on a laugh as she thought about how much she sounded like Joey.

With her head thrown against the headrest, she stared at the tree in her front yard. The broad green leaves shaded the rock landscaping, each one hanging from its own stem—alone. Just like her.

The engine turned over, and with tears still pooling in her eyes, she lifted her foot from the brake. The car coasted out of the driveway.

The feel of the gas pedal and dirty carpeting under her feet reminded her she had no shoes. Now what would she do? Driving the blocks of the neighborhood in a zig-zag pattern, she considered going home. But how would Derek learn what she faced every day if he never had to live it? No, she wouldn't go home, but what would she do without shoes?

With the car parked in the Walmart parking lot, Kat searched through her purse for her phone, hoping it wasn't dead. She'd forgotten to charge it—again. Her fingers touched the smooth screen, and she lifted it with one hand while wiping a tear away with the other. The sound of ringing echoed in her ear. *Come on, Mom, answer the phone.*

"Hello."

"Hi, Mom." She tried to keep her voice even, allowing her leg to sway side to side on her seat. "How's it going?"

"Fine."

Her mom never hurried into a conversation and never tried to lead one when Kat called.

"Good. What are you and Dad up to?"

"Not much. I baked a batch of cookies this morning. Dad's been eating them."

"Oh." She bit her lip. Kat tried to never talk to her mom about Derek, but this time she needed motherly comfort. "So, I ran out of the house today."

"Why?"

"Last night we took Joey to the baseball game, and when Derek changed his diaper, Joey spread poop all over everywhere. I guess it was on his clothes and the wall and everything. We had no extra clothes, and Derek was embarrassed, so we left. He's still mad."

"How do you know that?"

Kat's breath caught in her throat as she rolled her eyes. Why wouldn't she know when her husband was angry?

"He refused to help with Joey and gave me a hard time about making Joey more toast when he refused to eat what I'd already made."

"I wouldn't have made him more either."

Kat clenched and unclenched her free hand, and her leg changed motions, now bouncing up and down.

"If I don't, he'd starve."

"Kat, kids refuse food. Eventually, they eat what's available. Joey wouldn't let himself starve."

No words came to Kat's mind, just empty, dumbfounded space, for several long seconds.

"How did Derek refuse to help with Joey?"

Kat shook her head. "Instead of getting him from his room, he told me Joey was crying. I found Joey sitting in his chair with tears streaming down his red face. The chair was against the wall and couldn't rock. If he'd pulled the chair out, Joey would have stopped crying."

"Can't Joey move the chair?"

Kat's shoulders dropped, the conversation striking the same chord as the ones she'd had with Derek.

"No. He can push it, but he can't pull it."

"Honey, I know you go through a lot with Joey, and I get that some of it comes is from his condition, but not all of it, right?"

"Right."

"Well, what do the doctors say to do to help him?"

Her cheeks dampened again. "I don't know, Mom. Therapy starts tomorrow. Maybe then I can finally find out."

"Be patient. You don't want to make Derek upset. I read that a lot of couples with disabled kids get divorced."

Kat beat the air with her fist. "What am I supposed to do, let my husband live in his own little world while I take care of everything?"

Her mom's voice softened. "Of course not, but start with patience and go from there."

"Yeah... Mom, I gotta go. I'm sitting in a parking lot and need to get my errands done before Joey falls apart too much."

Kat hung up the phone. Didn't anyone understand the heartache she suffered from taking care of a child she couldn't understand? Why should she shelter Derek from his own son? Her shoulders hit the back of her seat, and she turned her head to look at the store. The idea to walk the mall and maybe indulge in a little shopping therapy of her own entered her mind, but for that she required shoes. Traversing the parking lot barefoot meant nothing. Her Arizona-toughened feet could handle it. How many people checked out people's feet anyway?

Dashing into the store, Kat rounded the corner to where they kept the large boxes of flip-flops. A blue pair landed on top of a green pair as Kat dug through the gigantic box of ninety-nine-cent shoes. Her lips tightened and she dropped her shoulders. The desire to wear plastic flip-flops had never existed in her life. With a determined look in her eye, she strolled directly to the shoe department and over to the sandals. At least there, bare feet were expected.

A set of slip-on sandals and a Kit Kat later, she drove out of one parking lot toward another. A small smile crossed her face. Chocolate helped everything.

The skylights in the mall brought a touch of the outside inside. She loved it. Kat strolled to an overstuffed, leatherette chair and dropped the bag of clothing she'd purchased for Joey at her feet. The Children's Place clearance racks filled his closet while emptying her wallet. To equalize the shopping trip out some, she'd also purchased a couple pairs of pants for Derek.

Lounging in the chair, she watched as other mall-goers strolled from one store to another. Mothers and fathers held the hands of their children who obediently did what they were told. Everyone wore smiles on their faces. One couple gathered their two young children into their arms and then gazed at each other as if they had no cares in the world. Who did that? Joey came to the mall for one reason: to melt down.

The last time she'd brought him, he wanted to keep playing at the indoor playground, but he'd already hit one kid and bitten another. When he'd flung his head into her nose, then refused to hold her hand, she'd let him walk alone. After he threw himself to the ground, she left him there—kind of. She'd walked away, then hid behind a curved wall in a small alcove.

Several people had tried to stop and help him, but she'd waved them away. Joey refused to move. He'd just lain there on the floor as if she were the problem.

Eventually, she doubled back and gathered him in her arms as he continued screaming. Now she wondered what had stopped him from running to the play area.

Maybe Derek had a point. Maybe she spent too much time babying him instead of teaching him. The thought didn't excuse Derek's behavior though. Still, affording forgiveness as they learned together seemed appropriate. Kat glanced at the time and sighed. Three and a half hours probably felt like an eternity to him.

Kat steeled herself for what she might find when she returned home.

Outside the house, silence pervaded. A good sign? She crossed her fingers. Easing the door open, she heard the TV playing cartoons. The plastic bags crinkled against the wall as she put them down, and Derek turned to greet her, a questioning concern in his eyes.

"Hi," she said.

"Hi."

"I'm sorry I ran off." She bit her lip.

"You okay now?"

"Yeah."

Derek nodded. "Good. You deserved a break."

Kat studied his face for a second, then ran over to the couch and landed between him and Joey, flinging an arm around each of them.

"I love my boys."

She turned back to Derek after tickling Joey.

"How did everything go here? Did you guys get lunch?"

Derek slowly nodded. "Sure did. We had peanut butter and jelly sandwiches."

Kat raised her brow and tightened her lips into a closed smile before speaking. "How did that go over?"

"Joey threw his sandwich on the floor and screamed for an hour and a half."

As Kat's jaw continued to drop, she reminded herself to close her mouth.

Derek smiled wanly. "Figured out he doesn't like jam."

She shook her head slowly. "Not at all."

"And he kept asking for a sun?"

"A circle. I cut his food into shapes. Sometimes he tells me what he wants by asking for things that are that shape. Like a sun." She held her shrug for a second before lowering her shoulder. "What did you do?"

"You mean after letting him cry for an hour and a half and watching him tear the sandwich into pieces before climbing off his chair and stomping on every bite-sized piece he'd thrown?"

"Yeah..."

"I sat him on the counter and constructed a peanut butter sandwich sans jam at the slowest pace possible. If he grunted, I tried something different. After the third one, I finally discovered what he wanted."

Laugh or cry? She wasn't sure, but when Derek brushed his hand over Joey's head and started laughing, Kat smiled. "I tried to tell you."

"Now you're going to play *I told you so*?" He poked her in the ribs. "I guess I really should listen to you more."

"Yes. Yes, you should." She laughed as she curled against his chest.

"And I shouldn't have let his turd painting bother me so much. After all, he's three."

A guffaw burst from Kat's throat. "That's an understatement, but I love you anyway."

Derek kissed the top of her head, tightening his arm around her.

The Test

Kat scrambled around the house trying to prepare for the meetings with several therapists. Dishes in the sink, blocks on the floor, crumbs on the couch! No matter how much she cleaned, another mess surfaced. Joey sat at the table eating his toast with a red motorcycle in his hand—another spoil of Kat's shopping therapy. She'd purchased three. What better way to make sure they never ran out of them again than to buy in bulk? She eyed Joey's plate. "Hurry up, Joey, we still need to put your shirt on."

Joey picked up his toast, studied it for a minute, and took a bite, ignoring Kat.

The first therapist, occupational therapy, would arrive anytime. Kat hurried into Joey's room and shuffled through his new clothes. Pulling out a knit shirt with a dinosaur on it, she stepped to her sewing kit, cut out the tag, and returned to the kitchen.

"Joey, I have a new shirt for you. The dinosaur is roaring."

She showed him the shirt, and he pushed it away, then took another bite of his toast.

"Let's put this on, okay? Your new friend Leah is coming over soon."

Joey glared at the shirt and growled.

Kat took a deep breath. "Come on, Joey, you don't even have pants on. Let's put a shirt on, please."

Joey climbed off the chair and spun the motorcycle wheel as he walked to the couch.

The doorbell rang.

With no other choice, Kat pushed the shirt over Joey's head and pulled his arms through, praying he'd cooperate. Instead, he threw his motorcycle across the room and started shrieking.

Great. Good job, Kat.

She ran to the door, leaving Joey, who had moved to the floor and started banging his head while crying.

"Hi." Kat smiled faintly. "You must be Leah."

A woman, only a few years younger than Kat, stood at the door holding a large bag and an exercise ball with a grin on her face.

"I am." She peeked around Kat. "Is that Joey?"

Kat opened the door wider, welcoming Leah into the house. "It is. He's a bit angry right now. It's my fault."

"Don't worry about it. That's why I'm here."

Kat closed the door and hurried over to Joey, picking him up. He squirmed to leave her arms, wailing louder, and she let him go.

Moving to the now crumpled dinosaur shirt thrown in the corner of the room, Kat said, "I'm sorry he's not dressed. I picked the wrong shirt today."

"He doesn't need to be dressed for me."

"Oh, okay."

Kat noticed the motorcycle on the floor, the handlebars broken. That's why Joey continued to scream. She rushed to the closet.

"Joey, do you need another motorcycle? I've got one right here."

Aware of Leah's eyes on her, Kat's hands trembled as she opened the box and handed the new toy to him.

"He loves these things, but they break so easily. And he's always throwing his toys, especially if I make him mad."

Leah smiled again. "That's pretty common. I have another idea that might help too."

Stepping behind Joey, Leah placed her hands at the top of his arms. With firm pressure, she squeezed both arms, then slid her hands down a few inches and squeezed again. She continued working her way down to Joey's wrists.

Kat sank onto the couch and watched. Joey's crying didn't stop but did soften. When he only whimpered, Leah leaned closer to his ear.

"Hi, Joey. My name's Leah. I'm your new friend. Do you see my ball over there? I like to play games with it. Do you want to play with me?"

Joey nodded and walked over to the ball.

Kat couldn't believe her eyes or ears. Joey never calmed down that easily.

"How did you do that?"

"It's called deep pressure. Kids with autism often struggle with either receiving too much sensory information or not enough. In either case, if something in their environment changes or isn't how they want it, they often melt down. Deep pressure helps calm their nerves so they can process information clearly again."

"You squeezed his arms?" Kat asked.

"Basically. You can do it too. Start at the top of his arms and work your way down toward his wrists. Move slowly and use a firm grip."

"I'll remember that."

She had no doubt she'd receive the opportunity to try the technique later that afternoon.

Leah sat down on the floor, a foot in front of Joey, and asked him for the ball. He looked warily in Kat's direction, and she repeated what Leah said. Leah smiled at her—a telling smile that said, *I'll take it from here.*

Kat smiled back, her leg bouncing as she tried to relax back onto the couch.

"Joey, please bring me the ball," Leah said again.

He lowered his head and glared at the wall from under hooded brows.

Kat pinched at a string she found lying on wound it around her finger, hoping Joey would do what Leah asked.

"Joey, let's play a game. Bring me the ball."

Joey swatted the ball toward Leah, and her face broke out in a grin.

"Great job! I'm going to roll it back, you catch it."

Each time Joey caught the slow-rolling ball, Leah scooted backward or to the side, forcing Joey to coordinate his actions with what he saw.

The last ten minutes of therapy, Leah had Joey lie on the floor, and she rolled the ball down his back to his feet. With each pass, Kat watch her son relax further.

"I read Joey's file. He has several meltdowns a day?"

Kat swallowed deeply. "Yeah. They can last for hours."

Leah nodded, and Kat realized the behavior didn't surprise her.

"When you see him getting upset, try using deep pressure like I showed you. If you have an exercise ball, he seems to like it too. The meltdowns won't stop, but I think you'll see a difference."

"Firm pressure?"

"Yup. You can also try noise-canceling headsets, like they use at shooting ranges, if noises are a problem."

Kat had read about those. "Do they really help? My husband thinks he should have to learn to deal with noise like everyone else."

"If he'll wear them, they can help, but your husband has a point. Eventually, you'll want him to learn to handle some noise. For now, I think they'd be okay to use."

Leah asked several more questions about Joey and his habits. Then she reached over and picked up the new motorcycle. "How many of these do you have stashed away?"

Kat ducked her head as she felt warmth trickle into her cheeks. "There are two more in the closet."

A gentle smile crossed Leah's face. "Try the deep pressure or other ways to divert his attention before giving him a new toy. That may stop the immediate problem, but it won't fix anything in the long run."

Kat nodded her understanding and walked Leah to the door.

"Hang in there, Mom," Leah said.

The door closed, and Kat leaned against it as a tear formed in her eye. The embarrassment of Joey's lack of clothing and his incessant wailing floated off her shoulders as she dreamed about ending meltdowns with deep pressure.

A speech therapist and a habilitation specialist also visited that day. Of course, this led to an exhausted household filled with transition meltdowns. But Kat wanted to get everything over with. Besides, some people claimed evaluations done during the child's worst times were best. Kat wasn't so sure. Either way, the three therapists seemed to get the information they needed.

The speech therapist, Emily, evaluated Joey and determined his needs fit mostly within the pragmatics category. Joey could speak, but he struggled with the communication aspect of language. Together, she and Kat decided regular sessions were best held on Tuesdays.

Kat learned that habilitation usually took place daily. The specialist, Nancy, explained that habilitation often worked best at the specialist's home. Kat struggled with the idea. Instead, Nancy would come to the house for three hours every weekday afternoon. She planned to help Joey potty-train, bathe, and use silverware. Nancy also explained that she provided respite as well.

"I'm here to give you and your husband a break. Think of me as a glorified babysitter."

Despite her exhaustion at the end of the day, Kat couldn't wait to tell Derek how the meetings with therapists had gone. Nancy planned to return tomorrow, while Leah and Emily would be back the following week.

That evening, Derek called and explained that he'd gotten stuck. A few servers never showed up, leaving the night manager short-handed. Derek agreed to stay until another server came in. He'd said a couple of hours, but when the squeaky door hinge woke her up, Kat realized time had slipped past closing.

"Hi, sweetie. Guess you didn't find anyone, huh?" A satisfying pop sounded as she stretched.

"We tried." Derek leaned over and kissed Kat on the forehead. "What are you doing up?"

"Waiting for you. I wanted to tell you about Joey's therapists."

Derek moved toward the fridge, and Kat followed behind, despite the living room bordering the kitchen. Pouring some juice into a glass, he asked, "Is he fixed?"

Kat rolled her eyes. "Derek, don't say things like that."

"Sorry." He tipped his glass of milk toward his opened mouth.

"So, we met his three therapists: Leah for OT—that's occupational therapy, Emily for speech, and Nancy for habilitation. You'll meet her tomorrow when you get home."

The words continued tumbling from her mouth as Derek brushed his teeth and climbed into bed. She finally stopped talking when he picked up his tablet to read. A smile crossed his face. "I'm glad you're happy."

Two days later, Kat unbuckled Joey from the car and held his hand as they strolled toward the school. She'd scheduled an appointment for testing with Exceptional Student Services, or ESS, a name she found odd for the special education department. Another surprise came when she'd discovered a medical diagnosis didn't immediately allow kids access to special education. Turned out, school districts had their own testing to determine whether or not a student's development was educationally delayed.

Though she'd read about the process some, the terms and varying opinions on the programs, in general, left her feeling woefully unprepared. However, the testing with the state had helped her to recognize one important factor—all questions required black or white answers. Joey either could or he couldn't. Acceptance to the preschool, that's what she aimed for.

The woman at the front office called back to a Mrs. Coach.

Kat fidgeted with Joey as they waited, combing her fingers through his hair and talking to him as she straightened his shirt. Then a plump lady with glasses hanging from around her neck appeared with a warm smile.

"Mrs. Burns?" The woman held out her hand. "I'm Mrs. Coach. If you and Joey will follow me, we can get started."

Kat counted her steps in sets of four during the silent walk down a short hall to a colorful classroom. A traditional preschool rug, rocking chair, and alphabet border greeted them as they entered.

"Mrs. Burns, this is Ms. Perry. She's the developmental preschool teacher here, and I'm the resource officer assigned to Joey. I also work with the elementary children through second grade," Mrs. Coach finally said.

"Hello." Kat shook Ms. Perry's hand, her own trembling.

"Hi, Joey." Ms. Perry lowered herself to Joey's level. "Can you look at me and say *hi*?"

Joey curled around Kat's leg and peered at the teacher from the side.

"I have some fun toys over here. Will you come play with me?"

She took Joey's hand and led him away from Kat. When he whimpered and dragged his feet, Kat stepped in his direction, but Ms. Perry met her gaze. "Don't worry, Mom. We'll be fine."

Mrs. Coach touched Kat's arm and gestured to a small u-shaped table in the corner. "It's a little short. Hopefully, you don't mind."

"Not at all."

"Today we're testing Joey to see if he qualifies for services. If he qualifies, then he'll be accepted into the developmental preschool. He seems like a pretty smart guy. He may not need anything."

Kat's heart pounded heavily in her chest. "He has autism, and I don't know..."

"I understand. Lots of kids have autism, but that's a medical diagnosis. We go off educational diagnoses here." She patted Kat's hand. "Don't worry, it's good if he doesn't qualify. That means he's educationally on track."

"I guess."

"We do have a few things to run through here. Did you bring the paperwork we sent you?"

Kat handed her the filled out paperwork that read similarly to the forms from the state.

"Perfect. Let me go score these real fast, and I'll be right back."

"Okay." Kat fiddled with a pen as she waited.

Joey had plenty of delays, but not cognitive ones. Now Kat worried he wouldn't qualify despite his need for socialization with kids his own age.

As Mrs. Coach scored the questionnaire, Kat let her eyes wander to where Joey "played" with Ms. Perry. The teacher currently struggled to get him to look at a picture book. She wanted him to point at a tree with a cat in it. Once done with the book, she asked Joey to trace some shapes and lines. He held the pencil in his fist instead of with the appropriate grip.

Mrs. Coach re-entered the room and sat at the table. "I can see he has some difficulties with certain areas dealing with anger and transitions, and the scores show he has some ASD tendencies."

"Tendencies? He's been diagnosed." Kat stared at the resource officer, confused.

"Yes, we can't say that because we aren't doctors."

"But the doctors have said it."

"Of course, and we take it into consideration."

What kind of testing were they doing? Kat rubbed her hands down her thighs as her leg started bouncing and nodded. "So does that mean—"

"We have to wait for Ms. Perry to finish, but it looks like she's getting close. If it's okay with you, we'd like to move right through the entire process today so you can leave knowing whether or not we can help your son."

"I—"

"It makes the process easier for all of us, and nothing changes. I'll just need you to waive your ten-day prior written notice."

"What does that mean?" Shallow breaths barely reached her lungs. Prior written notice? She'd read nothing about that.

"It means nothing more than we don't have to wait ten days before having a meeting."

Kat ignored the urge to count her heartbeats. "I guess we can do that."

"Good."

"If you'll sign here, we can get started."

Kat signed the paper. "Is Ms. Perry done?"

"She will be. Tell me, what kind of help do you think Joey needs from us?"

Warmth flooded Kat's face and ears as her heart pounded in her chest. Hadn't Mrs. Coach said they had to wait for Ms. Perry?

"The doctor says he needs OT and speech, as well as good socialization with peers from school."

"So that's what you're thinking, then? He's getting some help at home, right?"

Kat nodded. "Speech, OT, and hab."

"Good. We provide basic speech and OT, but getting the help through those service providers is better for Joey."

"I thought he needed both."

"Doctors like to say that, but it takes a lot to qualify for services like those here."

Ms. Perry joined them at the table, and Joey buried his head in Kat's side.

"He's a great kid. Super smart," Ms. Perry said.

Kat smiled. "He is smart, but he still has a hard time with some things."

"All kids do." Ms. Perry exchanged a smug look with Mrs. Coach.

Kat wondered if these teachers wanted to help Joey or if they wanted to see him disappear.

"Ms. Perry, would you like to share with Mom what you discovered while working with Joey today?" Mrs. Coach looked at her co-worker, a hollow smile plastered on her face.

"Sure. Like I said, Joey is super smart. He could count to one hundred and two, which surpasses most first graders, he knew fifteen letters, and could point at pictures with three items listed. Things like a picture with a table, chair, and plate. When he wanted to, he could follow two short directions, like stand up and touch your nose. But he's a little stubborn there."

Hearing the positive made Kat smile, but she didn't understand why the women focused on it so much. The negative was why they were there.

"How did he do with his small motor skills and his speech?" Mrs. Coach asked.

Ms. Perry moved her head back and forth as if she were considering. "He scored on the low side of average for both of them. Speech seemed lower in pragmatics, but the test we use only tests that lightly, not enough to tip the scales. I think he'd benefit from both OT and speech, but if he gets those at home, he wouldn't need much here."

"My understanding was that if he needed them, you had to provide them." Tension built in Kat's muscles, and she was certain the teachers planned to railroad her.

"Joey didn't score low enough to qualify for these services. It's a really good thing, Mrs. Burns. We don't want kiddos to need our help." Mrs. Coach had rushed to answer before Ms. Perry had the chance to speak.

Kat turned to Ms. Perry. "So you believe he needs these services?"

"Well"—the teacher swallowed deeply—"I believe he would benefit, but the scores are too high."

"We have to go off scores? Not what we think is best?" Kat asked.

"Not exactly. We have to prove he needs the help. We don't have any proof he needs it outside of his test results." Mrs. Coach shrugged, a forlorn look crossing her face.

Kat's breathing became more irregular as she considered their words. "What about the other areas?"

"I'm glad you asked," Mrs. Coach said. "I think we can agree that Joey struggles with eye contact. You've said he doesn't have much possibility to socialize with other kids—no daycare or organized play activities, is that correct?"

"Yes." Kat's nerves relaxed slightly.

"We do see that his social skill are delayed. Now, we usually aren't supposed to accept a child into the program for only socialization, but we agree that in Joey's case, it's necessary."

Tears welled in Kat's eyes. "Thank you."

Mrs. Coach and Ms. Perry smiled at her as Mrs. Coach continued. "Of course. We understand how difficult this process is for parents. And these kids deserve help. Our hands are often tied, but we do the very best we can for every single student, making sure they get what we are able to work out for them. A lot of times we wish we could do more."

The resource officer rustled some papers, and Kat wondered at her words. Somehow, they didn't completely match the actions, but Kat brushed it away. These women were helping her.

Mrs. Coach ran her pen across one of the pages. "We can offer two days a week of preschool. Do you need bus service?"

"Bus service?"

"The bus can pick Joey up at home and drop him off when school's over."

Kat bit her lip. "How many kids are on the bus?"

"Usually two or three. An aide rides on the bus with the students, and seat belts are provided. Safer than any car, really."

"O-okay."

"Perfect. Joey doesn't qualify for summer services, so he'll start in September when school starts up again."

"Great." Kat smiled as her nerves relaxed a little more. He'd get socialization. That mattered most.

"Meeting you and Joey has been a pleasure. I can't wait to work with him this fall." Ms. Perry patted Joey on the head as Kat gathered the newest pile of papers to file safely away with all the others.

Intruders

Derek turned the corner on his way home and slouched further into his seat at the sight of the red sedan. Nancy hadn't left yet. He swung his car door open and stepped into the never-ending summer heat, then paused at the front window and peeked inside. No one sat on the couch or played with blocks on the floor. An emptiness seeped into the pit of his stomach.

The squeak of the hinges brought no one running, and he glimpsed at the kitchen long enough to see Joey and Nancy sitting at the table. Joey attempted to scoop macaroni from his plate into his mouth but dumped most of it onto his lap.

The door to the computer room hung open, and he leaned against the jamb. Kat's body curved over the computer as she searched through what looked like drawings. A clip-art version of a toilet currently covered the screen. Her hair fell across her forehead, and she pushed it behind her ear. Derek smiled softly. If only it had been his fingers trailing across her skin.

"I'm home."

Kat startled slightly. "Hi, honey. I didn't hear you come in."

"It's hard to hear the door open from in here. What're you doing?"

She dropped her hand into her lap and turned in her chair to face him. "I'm preparing cards for Joey."

"With pictures of toilets on them?"

She wrinkled her nose. "This one will have that. I have one with a juice bottle, one with a cup of milk"—she flipped through the cards—"a sandwich, toys, and others." She shrugged. "I'm going to laminate them and hang them on a ring. Then we can communicate with him."

Derek shifted his weight. "With pictures? He understands words."

"This way he can show us a picture, and we can understand him."

"Isn't intruder number two teaching him how to speak?"

Kat rolled her eyes at him, but he couldn't help it. This therapy stuff was nothing more than a crazy medical trend.

"They're not intruders," Kat said.

"I feel like my house isn't even mine anymore."

Footsteps sounded in the hallway, and Derek moved into the room to make way for Nancy.

Kat's eyes shifted away from him to the hab specialist. "All done for the day?"

"Yup. He's bathed and has eaten dinner. We also worked on sitting on the potty, but I don't think he had to go."

"Great! I'll have these cards done by Monday."

Kat stood up and walked Nancy to the door, talking about their plans for Joey. She'd adopted every suggestion the therapists had given her, and every time Derek interacted with Joey, he worried Kat would correct him again.

Trying to shrug it off for the fifth time that week, Derek traipsed toward the kitchen and tripped over Joey's current line of blocks. The wailing began immediately. Derek picked up Joey and cringed as warm liquid gushed from under his hand.

"Kat."

The door closed, and Kat appeared at his side. "Come here, Joey, let's do some deep pressure."

"Kat, he peed."

"Oh. Will you get him clean underwear and shorts, while I start deep pressure for the meltdown? What happened anyway?"

"I tripped over his blocks. Aren't they teaching him not to line stuff up?"

Kat lowered Joey to his feet and gripped his arms, slowly moving her hands toward his wrists. "Not yet. I don't know how they do that."

Derek shook his head as he walked down the hall to gather the clothing Kat had asked for. So far, the therapists hadn't taught Joey to communicate, hold a spoon, or stop lining things up, but they had confiscated his diapers. Success. He smirked.

Returning to the living room, he recoiled as urine ran down Joey's leg and puddled on the floor. He'd peed a second time.

"I don't think he's ready for potty training. Can't we put a diaper on him?"

"Nancy wants us to try underwear for a bit. She's potty-trained four of her own children. I'm sure she knows what she's doing."

"Were her kids autistic?"

Kat rolled her eyes again. "Does it matter? She still knows more than we do."

Giving up, Derek flopped onto the couch and snapped up the TV remote.

"Derek?" Kat's voice softened, becoming a tone that usually meant she wanted something.

He gave her a sideways glance.

"Do you think we could leave that off?"

He hurled the remote back to the couch. "Sure. Are we having dinner, or should I figure that out too?"

"Joey and I have eaten. I put some macaroni in the fridge for you if you want it." Kat continued helping Joey into his fresh clothes with an impassive expression despite his raucous wailing.

Derek stood up. "Never mind."

He wasn't hungry anyway.

The wailing continued for the next hour. Derek ground his teeth as he tried to ignore the noise. Two servers had quit, a customer blew up at him over a correctly prepared order, and his wife showed no interest in him.

He told himself Kat would calm down and everything would return to normal. After all, it had only been a month of intrusions, and Joey started preschool soon. She'd relax once she got used to him being gone for a little bit. Besides, Derek could handle more than a month.

Opening the drawer to his nightstand, he picked up the last two foam earplugs and pushed them into his ears.

A couple of hours later, Kat wandered into the room and toppled onto the bed. Derek noticed her lips moving and removed one earplug then the other.

"What?"

"That was long."

"Isn't that pressure stuff supposed to stop the meltdowns?"

She cuddled into his shoulder. "Not completely. And not right away."

"Were you squeezing his arms the whole time?"

She sighed. "No. I tried some joint compressions and brushing too, but nothing worked."

He reached up and swept the hair off her face, her silky skin sending tingles into his fingertips as he breathed in the aroma of her shampoo.

"Has it ever?"

"It worked for Leah when she showed it to me."

"A month ago?"

She curled in closer, her heart beating against his chest. "Yeah."

Shifting his weight, Derek pulled her closer and kissed her neck. Despite seeing Kat daily, he missed her.

"Derek?"

"Hmm?" He pushed her nightgown off her shoulder.

"I'm really tired. Do you mind if..."

He stopped, flinging both arms behind his head as he glowered at the ceiling. She rubbed his chest, obviously aware of his opinion. But it didn't matter. Frustration had already filled the emptiness his passion left behind.

School shoppers crowded the aisles of every store Kat and Joey entered. This time, she glanced down at her son and exhaled sharply. The school-supply list arrived with plenty of time to shop, but supplies didn't go on sale until the week before classes started. With all the therapies and additional reading she'd been doing, time had slipped away.

Now, school started tomorrow, and Joey had nothing. Even worse, she had to locate school-approved clothing he would wear. Navy or khaki bottoms in a soft fabric weren't the easiest to find when athletic shorts weren't allowed.

On top of that, some items on the list made little sense. She understood the crayons and safety scissors. Index cards easily became flash cards. But a box of tissue and a ream of paper? And how many pocket folders did a preschooler really need? Eight seemed excessive. No matter. She'd provide what they asked for. Rocking the boat before kindergarten? Probably the less-effective choice.

As Kat reached for folders, one blue, four red, two green, and a yellow, Joey tossed his head onto the cart's handle and shrieked. Heads turned as curious shoppers gawked at them.

"What happened, Joey?" Kat scrutinized the area around her son.

Nothing appeared out of place. Then she scanned the floor. A package of pencil erasers rested next to the cart's wheel.

"How did you get those?" She picked them up. "Where'd these come from? You don't need erasers."

Searching the cardboard bins, she found one filled with erasers and glue sticks next to the construction paper. The unneeded erasers landed in the box, and Joey wailed louder.

"We're not buying those."

A woman coming from the opposite direction smiled at Kat, then leaned over to Joey. "Stop fussing." She glimpsed at Kat. "How old is he?"

"Three."

"Three?" she narrowed her eyes at Joey. "You know better than to cry like that in a store."

Kat's heart thudded. *One, two, three, four...* She pushed her cart further down the aisle, doing her best to ignore the current meltdown, if that's what it was. Didn't all three-year-olds scream when Mom took things away?

When Joey's shoe hit a passerby after he'd ripped it from his foot, Kat decided they had enough supplies. The eight-pack of washable markers would have to do instead of the ten, especially since that's all the three stores she'd visited had.

The morning light shone through Joey's bedroom window, and Kat shook his little body. "Come on, time to wake up and get ready for school."

His eyes fluttered open before closing again.

"Hey, don't you want to ride the school bus?"

This time, Joey sat up and curled into Kat's arms as he nodded.

"I thought so. You'll love it. It has big windows you can see out of, and all the cars look super little." She picked him up. "Let's get you some toast."

Kat watched Joey wake up a little more as she made his breakfast. Her three-year-old was too little for school.

She rolled her shoulders back and stood taller. He needed it. School would help. Everyone said so. She'd have to get over the fear of him riding a bus and melting down where no one understood him.

Her lip quivered.

"I can do this," she muttered to herself.

When Joey finished eating, they hurried to get him dressed. The excitement of riding the bus helped Joey stay on task, and she reminded him of the impending adventure often. Five minutes before the scheduled time, they stepped outside and to the curb.

Though early September, the never-ending heat and monsoon had yet to disappear and pushed against Kat as she held Joey's hand. She wiped at her forehead and neck, wishing the heat were drier. The slightly higher humidity in the air managed to stop perspiration from doing any good, no matter what others claimed.

As the bus rumbled down the street, Joey attempted to let go of Kat's hand to run forward.

Bending down, she turned him to face her. "Is it okay to run into the street?"

Joey looked past her toward the bus.

She cupped his chin with her hand until his eyes met hers. "Joey, is it okay to run into the street?"

His little brow creased as he narrowed his eyes and pushed at her hand.

"Is it okay to run into the street?"

"No," he growled.

Kat let go of his chin and smiled. "Right. Hold my hand. It's coming."

His eyes brightened as he stared down the street.

Stopping with a jolt, the bus came to rest in front of them and the doors slid open. Joey dashed forward.

"Don't run!" Kat and an aide yelled at the same time.

The aide reached down, took his hand, and helped him climb the tall stairs into the bus. Kat exhaled, her arms crossed over her belly, and allowed her leg to bounce three times.

"All set, Mom. We'll drop him off at ten forty-three."

The aide and driver waved, and Kat searched for Joey's smiling face in the window. The top of his head barely reached the bottom.

I can do this.

The squeak of the closing door announced her presence to the empty house. Silent digital clocks refused to tick. The constant flow of the air conditioner made no sound. Not even a faucet dripped. Kat dragged her feet to the couch and turned on the TV. The blaring only upset her more.

Swinging her purse onto her shoulder, she rushed out the door and into the car. Every bone in her body desired nothing more than to follow Joey to school. But she couldn't. Not when school was what he needed, and it was.

Instead, she drove to the nearest grocery store. With a house regularly depleted of real food, why not?

Perusing the aisles, Kat picked up certain items, and read the product descriptions of others. The automatic-timed stirrer caught her attention. Derek made great soups and sauces. In time, she placed it back on the shelf. The amount of cooking he did had dropped significantly, and she doubted he'd pick it up again anytime soon.

With the cart full of food, Kat pushed it to her car and loaded the trunk. Two days. Joey would go back to school in two days. The idea taunted her as she unloaded the groceries at home.

The help Joey received at school could mean the difference between him attending a normal class or a self-contained class when he was older. Early intervention meant a better life. Employment versus unemployed. Functional versus nonfunctional. But did he have to ride the bus?

Things happened on buses. Students bullied each other. Bus drivers yelled. Kids got off at the wrong stop.

She clutched her sides.

All of that was true, but none of it reflected the type of bus Joey rode. No more than three kids. Seat belts. An aide. He'd be fine. It's why she allowed him on the bus in the first place.

A horn sounded outside at 10:40 a.m. Kat ran into the heat, leaving the door wide open. The bus doors slid to the sides, and Joey's short legs dropped from one tall step to the next. A construction-paper hat topped his head, and a grin brightened his face.

"Did you have fun?"

He nodded. "Joey blue hat."

"I see that. It's a nice blue hat, isn't it?"

He nodded again.

His little hand slipped into hers, and she led him inside.

"Did you like the bus?"

"Uh-huh."

The backpack, with a single notebook inside, dropped to the floor, and Joey ran to the shelf filled with his toys.

A pull of the bag's zipper and Kat examined the notebook. The words *Joey had a great first day* had been written on top of a calendar square and scribbled over with green crayon, each scribbled line passing over the printed ones.

The clacking of blocks on the floor rang in Kat's ears as the normal feel of the house returned.

Even though Joey had started school more than a month ago, Derek continued to come home to the same scene. Nancy and Joey in the kitchen eating as

Kat read up on some new way to help their son. He assumed things would get better once Joey started school, but now he wondered about the school as much as the therapists. According to Kat, the developmental preschool gave Joey a chance to play with other broken kids. But as far as Derek could tell, Joey still rarely cared about playing with anyone, especially others his own age. Maybe he'd learn his ABCs.

Either way, Kat hadn't relaxed and continued showing more interest in autism fixes than him. It wasn't right.

Moreover, Joey kept screaming. And as for gripping Joey's arms or burying him under pillows—it never worked when Derek tried. However, Kat said it often worked for her preemptively. Not that preemptive did anything when Joey screamed his head off.

Something had to change.

Work went about as well as home. Derek worked one Saturday a month, and tonight, once again, he found himself short on servers. He might as well work at a fast-food hamburger joint for all the service his customers received. It was just part of the industry, but it still sucked.

As the dining room filled to capacity, Derek grabbed an order pad and set himself up with a few tables.

Soon, a family of six sat in his area, and he introduced himself. A boy of fourteen or fifteen cuddled into his mother's side, and she spoke to him quietly before handing him a large headset.

Kat had mentioned getting Joey a headset, but Derek had no intention of his kid looking like this one. Joey had to learn to deal with noise.

Forcing a smile, Derek asked for their order. Dad asked for more time, and Derek agreed. He liked to check with the customers quickly, even when most needed extra time.

As he gathered plates from one table and delivered a bill to another, he kept tabs on the family, trying to determine when to return. Once the menus were set aside, he strode over to take their order. Three kids' burgers, a kids' chicken strips, and two Arizona Melts with fries.

Although the orders kept the kitchen busy, the cooks managed to complete them fast, and a short time later, Derek returned to the family of six with their food. The boy sprawled across the bench, kicking his feet into the padded cushion while flicking his fingers together. Derek wondered if he was like Joey. Setting a burger in front of him, Derek smiled at the parents, asked if they needed anything more, and then left.

Only moments passed before chaos stormed at the family's table. Looking over, Derek watched the boy chuck the plate across the table, his dad catching it with deft hands. Derek hurried over.

"Is everything okay? Is there something wrong with his food?"

The mother pressed her hands down the boy's arms in a pattern Derek recognized, and he determined to pay closer attention. Maybe this kid would calm down faster. He was older.

The mother smiled sadly. "I'm sorry. We didn't know the bun had sesame seeds on it. He won't eat those."

"Let me take it back and see what we can do for you."

In the kitchen, Derek asked for a fresh kids' burger with two bottom buns. He couldn't hear the screaming after a few minutes. Had the pressure thing worked? As he strode to check on his tables, he took the order of an elderly couple and visited the family again. The mother and son were gone, and the other four ate silently.

"Can I get you anything more? That burger should be ready in about two minutes."

The father lifted a corner of his mouth. "Thanks. My wife took him outside for a bit."

"No problem. My son has a hard time with his food too."

Under his breath, Derek promised himself no teenager of his would throw a fit in public over sesame seeds.

As the mother and son returned to the table, Derek brought the new burger and placed it in front of the boy.

Barely raising his head, the boy glared at the burger and lobbed his head back against the bench, kicking at the underside of the table. The mother moved, and the father, who had finished his meal, took their son's hand and helped him back outside.

Derek stood there, trying to determine what to do. He'd dealt with young kids' tantrums several times in the restaurant, some a little older, but never a teenager.

"Sorry, he's had a hard day," the mother said as she gave Derek another apologetic smile.

"Hey, we all have those, right? Would you like me to box this up for you?"

The woman hesitated. "No. He won't eat it. Thank you anyway."

Derek grumbled as he removed the boy's burger from the family's bill. Two burgers completely wasted, and he only had so much he could comp before corporate started asking questions.

That pressure stuff did nothing to stop the meltdown, either. It was another example of how this nonsense Kat insisted on had no point. A medical trend, nothing more. Joey had better not act like that much longer. He needed to talk to Kat.

That night, Derek waited in bed for his wife to finish putting Joey down. The boy slept in a rocking chair, and tonight he screamed so much at bedtime his cries had become hoarse.

Knowing Kat couldn't handle leaving Joey in his room alone when he cried, Derek worked to stay awake by watching videos and reading. He slipped into the activity easily. Despite having given up on waiting for Kat the last couple of months, the previous habit still felt normal.

News headlines scrolled across his screen, and he chose one without paying attention to what it said. The crying had stopped several minutes previous, and he suspected Kat would come in before he finished reading the article. A split second later, as expected, he heard his wife shuffle into the hallway and quietly close Joey's door. But the shuffling footsteps headed in the wrong direction.

He waited patiently, then a light flicked on at the other end of the house. What was she doing? Climbing out of bed, Derek grabbed his pants off the edge of the laundry hamper and left the room in search of his wife.

Kat sat on the couch eating an apple and watching TV. How many other nights had she stayed up without him?

Leaning against the living room entryway with his arms crossed, Derek waited for Kat to notice him. When she finished the apple and fluffed a pillow, he gave up.

"The bed's more comfortable."

Kat startled and paused the TV. "I thought you were asleep."

"Nope. Watched you eat that entire apple."

She nodded. "It was pretty tasty."

Derek walked to the couch and sat at the opposite end.

"How often do you come watch TV when I'm in bed?"

She swallowed. "Most nights."

"Why?"

"You're usually asleep and..." her words fell away.

"I waited up for you tonight."

"Oh... Why?"

Derek exhaled and gazed at Kat as he gathered his thoughts. Dang, he missed holding her. He scooted closer and took her hand.

"I miss you."

She tilted her head, with a confused look in her eyes.

"I haven't gone anywhere."

A faint smile crossed his lips, and he tried again. "I ended up serving again tonight. A family sat at one of my tables, and they had a son, fourteen maybe fifteen, who tossed his food across the table. The bun had sesame seeds."

He stared deeper into her eyes—so beautiful. "He had a major tan...meltdown, and when I served him a new burger, the whole thing started over."

Her face dropped. "That poor boy. I'm glad you were there to help."

"Kat, he had a tantrum over sesame seeds. No one can taste them. His mother had to take him out after the first burger. By the time the second burger was ready, his dad had finished eating, and he took the boy out. The kid didn't take a single bite of food—not even a fry."

Kat's jaw tightened. "What are you saying?"

"The parents couldn't eat at the same time. They had nothing to do with each other because of the meltdown. The mom tried that deep pressure stuff. It didn't work."

"How terrible. That poor family."

He gazed at her, his mouth searching for his next words. "I don't want that."

He clung to her hand.

"I don't want that either, but Joey's learning. He's learned to show me the juice or the milk card when he wants a drink."

"Great." Derek's shoulders dropped. "Is there a card for no sesame seeds?"

Kat rolled her eyes again. He hated it when she rolled her eyes—his questions were valid.

"No, there's no card for that."

"Look, I just...do you really think this therapy stuff is working? I feel like a stranger in my own home. And I miss you."

"Everything I've read says therapy will help. Everything." She shook her head. "Why do you keep saying you miss me, anyway?"

Derek scooted closer and wrapped his arms around her. The soft aroma of her hand-pressed soap wafted toward him. "We don't have *us* time anymore. Or we haven't for a long time."

Kat laughed. "If you want sex, you need to stay awake or wake up earlier. It's kind of a prerequisite."

"Wow." Derek grinned. "Yeah, that would be nice, but I don't mean just that."

The confused look passed across Kat's face again.

"Kat, since Joey's diagnosis, everything has been about Joey. Doctor's visits, therapists, new ways to help him learn. I come home from work and intruder number three is here—"

"Derek, please. I've asked you not to—"

"I'm sorry. I just feel like everything is about Joey. What time do we have together?"

"I can ask Nancy to come earlier, but I think she has another client around lunchtime, and learning to use silverware is one of Joey's goals."

"And tonight, he still dumped most of his food down himself. I noticed he's back in diapers too. At least that's an improvement."

He scooted back from Kat as he tried to bridle his frustration.

"This is an odd way to ask me to spend time with you." Kat exhaled sharply. "What do you want me to do? Stop therapy? Because I won't. No way. My biggest priority right now is Joey, and yours should be too."

His eyes met hers. "Should it? Because I thought that was you." The anguished words brushed past his lips.

Kat bowed her head. "I'm a priority too, but when you're a parent, your child's needs come first."

She took his hand and squeezed it gently. "I love you, and I know how hard this is. It's hard for me too. But, Derek, we have to do this together."

"Yeah." He swallowed, uncertain the talk had accomplished anything. "Do you think Nancy could watch Joey for a couple of hours this week? We could go out. That's part of her job, right?"

Kat's tongue clicked at the top of her mouth as she held her breath, a sign she'd stopped herself from saying something. "I'll talk to her."

She scooted closer and wrapped his arms around her waist, then gazed into his eyes. "Now about bed..."

Wednesday afternoon, Kat reminded herself to ask Nancy about staying late Friday night or coming sometime Saturday to watch Joey. She'd forgotten the last two days, and Derek kept asking her if they had plans or not. If she forgot again, a family mutiny could ensue.

She pulled Joey onto the couch. "Hi. What's your name?"

The game hadn't changed much, but a look crossed his face as he beamed at her.

"I know your name. Your name is George."

Joey shook his head.

"You're not George? Then what is your name?"

He didn't answer, but fixed his eyes on hers, waiting for her to speak again.

"I know your name." The doorbell rang, so Kat hurried to the end of the game "Your name is David."

Joey smiled. "I not David. I Joey!"

"You're Joey! I love you, Joey!"

Kat gave him a big hug as she carried him to open the door for Nancy.

As the door swung wide, Kat's heartbeat raced. How could she trust anyone to watch Joey? The only sitter he'd ever had was her mom, and she lived too far away to have regularly.

Nancy rushed inside and took Joey from Kat, placing him on the floor.

"You really should stop carrying him everywhere. Let him walk."

Kat rubbed her hands down her legs. "It's easy to forget."

The hab specialist grinned as she bent down to look Joey in the eyes, who shifted his gaze to the side.

"Joey, where are your cards?"

"I have those. He threw them at me earlier and started to rip them from their ring, so I took them away."

Kat ran out of the room and retrieved the cards from the top of the refrigerator. "Here you go."

Nancy took the cards and flipped to the one with the toilet on it, then showed it to Joey. "Do you have to go potty?"

Joey spun away from her and plopped himself on the floor in front of his blocks.

"He'll point at the juice or milk cards for me now," Kat offered.

"That's good. The small steps count."

Nancy returned her attention to Joey, and Kat stood by the side, her knee bouncing awkwardly. When a break in the one-sided conversation between Nancy and Joey appeared, she jumped in. "Nancy, my husband wants to go out on Friday."

"What a wonderful idea. We haven't used any of your respite hours."

"So, you're available?"

"Did you have a specific time frame in mind?"

Kat shifted on her feet. "After hab for two or three hours?"

"I'll plan on it, but next time, try to give me a week's notice. My other clients like Friday nights too."

"Of course," Kat stammered.

Nancy returned to her work with Joey, excusing Kat from the room.

In the office, Kat read her usual websites. How did other parents leave their children? The question still hammered at her insides. She yearned for calm and meltdown-free time, but Derek hadn't seen Joey much in the last several months either. The fact that work kept him so busy with overtime didn't help the problem any. And Derek's jealousy of Joey only confused her more. A parent jealous of their child? How?

After posting on a social media autism parent-support group about respite, she researched movies and restaurants. Somehow, the typical date lacked luster. Searching through several Phoenix attraction articles helped little. The temperatures ranged low enough for outside activities now, and she considered possibilities. Goofy-golfing? It left time for conversation, but didn't last so long that she would worry about Joey. She might enjoy riding the roller coaster again too.

Friday evening, Kat brushed the tears out of her eyes as she chose her outfit for the night. Spending some time away from the mayhem of home sounded great in theory, but her exhaustion left her wanting nothing but a pile of Kit Kats and her bed.

From morning to afternoon, Joey had meltdowns about clothing, food, and his bath, which she'd listened to as Nancy bathed him. To add insult to injury, he'd discovered screwdrivers and unscrewed his bedroom door from the lower hinge. Once he'd recovered from the meltdown following the removal of the screwdriver from his hand, he snuck a butter knife from the kitchen drawer and did it again. The door now hung by the upper hinge, no longer latching properly.

The appealing thought of canceling the date had occurred to Kat, but Derek's excitement had grown with each passing day. And if she didn't stop crying soon, she'd end up looking like a red-faced raccoon.

The sound of the front door opening brought Kat's head up. Snagging the first blouse she saw, one with a single ruffle at the neckline running down the front, she brushed the last tear away and hurried to get dressed. Her left foot slid into her new favorite sandals as she left to meet Derek in the hall.

"Hi, sweetie," she said.

Derek wound his arms around her waist and brought her body closer to his. Leaning down, he met her lips. Stale burgers wafted to her from his clothing, and she ended the kiss early.

"Why don't you change before we go."

"Absolutely. I might even shower." Derek flashed a gleaming grin. "I'll hurry."

The stinging prick returned to Kat's eyes and she blinked, working to keep the tears at bay. Crying had no purpose.

She loved her husband. She loved her son. But at some point, she had to take care of herself. When would that time come? Sitting on the couch, she crossed her arms and hugged herself. It was uncanny how many of the techniques intended for Joey helped her. Glad Nancy and Joey were in his room, she walked into the master bedroom.

Derek exited the shower, and Kat's heart sank. The idea of seeing him swathed in a towel used to excite her, now it wore her out.

Guilt surged within her veins. Derek loved her. Of all the things he complained about, the biggest was wanting more time with her. But shouldn't he want to spend time with Joey too?

Reflecting on their last meaningful conversation, she couldn't fathom putting anyone but her child first. Still, she needed to make time for Derek, right? But what about her?

The notion rammed itself into her consciousness before she could stop it. No one suggested she not take time for herself. She just had to do it. With Joey at preschool two days a week, she had time to shop for groceries and clean the house alone. That was different. It should be enough, but it wasn't.

"I'm about ready." Derek called from the bathroom as he applied a small amount of cologne.

"Great." Kat eased off the bed to stand by his side.

Grasping her hand, he pulled her into his arms. She breathed in the fresh cologne. "You smell amazing."

With another deep breath, she snuggled deeper into his chest.

"Glad you like it."

"Maybe if you hold me like this a bit longer, I'll make it through the rest of the day."

"What? We're going out, right?"

"Mm-hmm. It's just been a long day."

Derek nodded and tightened his arms around her. "I can give you another minute or two."

Crushed Wishes

Hand in hand, Derek led Kat from the car to the giant blue castle-shaped building. A large arcade rested inside its walls while mini golf, bumper boats, and the roller coaster of Kat's childhood mingled with other attractions outside, bringing excitement to the crowd—both young and old. A twinkle brightened Kat's reddened eyes as she pointed out all the memories and differences before them. The party room had changed colors, but the hedges dividing the mini golf courses still held the same square shape. Derek pulled her closer and she giggled, a sound he'd longed to hear for months.

She'd been crying when he got home, and he'd worried she'd cancel. But now, after a long day at work, spending time with Kat, without concern of meltdowns or new-found information regarding the cause of autism, brought buoyancy to his step.

"Four courses. Which is the best?" Derek asked Kat.

"I don't remember." She shrugged with a smile. "My friends always chose. I remember a windmill."

Derek chuckled. "You can't have a mini golf course without a windmill."

Kat scanned the four courses. "I've only seen one. But if we skip the eighteenth hole we can play all four courses and figure out where it is."

She took her green ball from his hand and placed it on the brown mat.

"Hey, wait," he said as his eyes scanned her, "do that again."

"Do what? Lean over?"

He raised his eyebrow and the corner of his mouth to answer her question.

Kat grinned as she shook her head, eyeballed the distant crowd, and bent over to adjust her ball one more time.

The dented club whacked the edge of the ball, which rolled three feet to the left and stopped. The air soon carried that infectious giggle Derek loved so much.

"It's been a long time," she said as she moved out of his way.

Derek held his club at eye level and peered down it, lining it up with the hole from where he stood on the mat.

"Hole in one, here I come."

Smacking his ball, he watched as it ran over a hump and off to the right, landing several feet and two hills away from his mark.

"I'm thinking eighteen holes is about right," Kat said.

There was that beautiful giggle again.

Eventually, conversation turned from banter to that of a married couple discussing life. Derek told Kat the restaurant gossip and shared a few crazy customer stories like he used to. Kat mostly spoke of Joey. He watched as her shoulders lost a little height and her step lost a little bounce. Her day had been hard. Maybe she needed to get out as much as he did.

"I thought his meltdowns were getting better?"

She hit her next ball, watching it jump the concrete and land near a bush. "Most days. But now he's learned to remove his bedroom door, so..."

"Yeah."

Amusement colored his voice, and Derek recognized the flowing ribbon of pride for his son running through his mind. He hadn't felt that so strongly in some time.

"You can't question his abilities," he said.

"I'm glad you're amused, because you get to fix it and figure out a way to keep him out of the silverware drawer."

"Why don't you get a lock for it?"

"Like the one I took off a year ago because he kept opening it so he could line the silverware up through the house?"

Derek tapped his ball into the hole in seven strokes. Something had changed with Kat's last comment. Glancing in her direction, he caught her biting her lip. He sidled up closer and ran his hands down her arms.

"I'll figure something out," he said.

Kat's phone rang. He dropped his arms and stepped back as Joey's terrifying scream leaped from the phone's earpiece toward him. Great. His wife's face paled until tears bubbled in her eyes and threatened to overflow. A fist formed at his side. One night. All he wanted was one single night.

"We'll be right there," Kat said as she hung up and turned to Derek. "We have to get Joey to the hospital or urgent care if there's one open."

"What happened now?" He tried to control the bite to his voice.

Kat hurried toward the eighteenth hole to put away her ball and club, tears streaming down her face. Her mouth opened to speak, but nothing came out.

"Kat. Stop."

He rushed to her and held her close. "What happened?" This time, the frustration eased and his voice softened.

Shoving him, she continued her journey, her body shaking uncontrollably.

"Joey was pushing the step stool to the counter to help Nancy, and it closed on his hand." Her composure broke. "What was Nancy thinking? Why didn't she see that his hand was between the bars and not on the step? She says his fingers were flattened, and his middle finger has a gash."

She lobbed her ball into the return hole and flung her arms down to her sides. "This is my fault. I shouldn't have left him. I knew better."

Derek followed, letting her fume. After her day, she needed a release, so he bound his inner torments and kept them from escaping.

One night, and it had been going so well. Now he'd waste time in a hospital with a screaming kid. Why did he bother?

"Kat, slow down. We'll get there, and he'll be fine."

"Fine? He could have several broken fingers. He is not fine."

Once in the car, Derek paid close attention to his wife's mood while he struggled with his own. Kat fidgeted, adjusting her position every few minutes, her knee shaking wildly. Under her breath, she muttered, "Leave him with someone else... never again."

The words struck Derek harder than he expected.

"Kat, accidents happen. I had stitches and broken bones as a kid. He'll survive."

"Don't. Just...don't."

Derek clenched his mouth shut. Evidently, silence and driving were his responsibilities, and he took them seriously.

After rolling into the driveway, he waited in the car until Kat came out carrying a screaming Joey in her arms.

Nancy followed close behind. "Kat, I'm so sorry this happened."

"I'm sure you are. You should have been watching closer. Go ahead and leave now. I'll call the agency and find someone else to work with Joey from now on."

Derek swallowed deeply as he clenched his jaw tighter before Kat caught him gawking. With Joey wailing in the back, and Kat sitting infuriated next to him, he backed out of the driveway.

"Where am I going?" he asked.

"There's a twenty-four hour urgent care about five miles down the road. Head west."

Questions raced through Derek's mind—but asking now—bad idea. Running to urgent care when all he wanted was to finish their date wasn't his idea of fun, and for the first time in several months, he saw the benefit of all these therapists and specialists. Now, Kat had fired the only one capable of staying with Joey as a babysitter? Why? Because Joey got hurt the same way kids get hurt every day?

Risking a glance at Kat, his heart sank. Too much anger emanated from her.

Derek carried Joey into the urgent care and tried to comfort him. Unfortunately, he rarely managed to comfort Joey. This time he imagined himself trying to pet an angry pit bull.

The chair squeaked as he sat down. "Let me see your hand, buddy."

Joey ignored Derek and continued screaming, but Derek carefully took his son's wrist in his hand, and lifted the cloth wound around it. Each of his four fingers showed a flat space running their width on the pads of the fingers to below the first joint. Could bones flatten without breaking? His middle finger had torn open at the pad, the edges of the wound somewhat jagged. Deep.

Guilt for his recent ruminations flooded through him. Joey was hurt and needed help.

Sometimes he wondered if Kat understood him. He loved their son as much as he loved her, but Derek didn't know how to control his disappointments or anxieties the same way she did hers, and she held it against him. But their relationship didn't matter right then. Instead of worrying about Kat, he determined to help Joey. Those fingers had to hurt.

"Ouch. It'll be okay, buddy. The doctor will fix you up."

As he wrapped the cloth back around Joey's fingers, he noticed the blood stains. Joey must have noticed too, because his screaming lessened as his focus changed.

"Hey, bud. You're doing great! You cut your finger open pretty good, huh? Did the stool fold up on you?"

Joey nodded and protected his injured hand with his good one.

"Nancy helped you though, right?"

"She could have helped more by not letting him push the stool." Kat slid into the chair next to them and brushed her fingers down Joey's face.

"He's pushed that stool around plenty. We've let him do it," Derek said.

"We're the parents. As a professional, she should have been more careful."

Kat took Joey from Derek, held him on her lap and enveloped him with both of her arms, her head close to his.

"That's ridiculous," he muttered the words under his breath, but not soft enough.

"What's ridiculous about it? Higher standards are always expected from professionals."

He clenched his teeth, refusing to respond. The fact that Joey had been injured pelted at him, but Nancy hadn't caused it. He couldn't blame her when the whole situation could have happened with any adult.

"Come on, Derek. I've always watched where he put his hands on that stool for this very reason."

His pulse twitched along his jawbone.

"We never should have left him," she said.

"Yes, we should have." The words burst out of him.

Her gaping eyes met his, and Kat's pursed lips parted, preparing to speak or bite his head off. He wasn't sure which.

"Kat, we can't be a family if the two of us never spend time together. I saw you tonight. You'd had a terrible day. You'd been crying for Pete's sake, but when we got to that giant blue castle, your whole demeanor changed."

"It did not. I faked it for you."

"You're lying." Derek slouched further in his chair. "I know when you're faking."

Kat snorted. "Sure."

An old woman with a swollen toe watched them through sideways glances, and Derek had no intention of giving her more of a show. Instead, he folded his arms and waited an hour in silence for the slow urgent care to call Joey's name.

After strapping Joey into the back seat, Kat slipped into the spot next to him. The x-rays showed no break, but watching Joey receive a shot from a giant needle and get three stitches in his tiny finger broke her heart.

It never should have happened. How Derek didn't understand that was beyond her. Yeah, Joey had pushed the stool from place to place before, but it had never caught on the floor or a toy, or whatever it was that it caught on, and closed.

Why on earth did Derek feel the need to go out anyway? She let her folded arms relax some, dropping her shoulders. She'd had fun going out until her phone rang. The problem was Nancy. Joey might melt down a lot, but keeping track of him wasn't difficult. He stayed in the same room, and it's not like Nancy had four or five kids to take care of. One. Only Joey—not hard at all.

The day needed to end.

She peered at Joey. His little hand had plumped back out. Even the doctor seemed surprised no fingers had broken. She couldn't imagine the pain of getting fingers stuck like that in the first place. The notion of getting the fingers unstuck sent a shiver down her spine.

Tracing his face, she determined it didn't matter what it took, her little boy would never go through something so traumatizing again.

Still, habilitation helped Joey more than she wanted to admit. He screamed through his baths, but his grip on the silverware had tightened and more food found its way into his mouth. Potty training seemed never-ending, but one day that would change. She was sure of it.

She decided she'd request a new hab specialist first thing in the morning, but she had no intention of using respite hours ever again.

Kat found herself waking to a gentle shake of her shoulder.

"We're home, Kat. Go to bed. I've got Joey."

Derek's words were kind, but his voice held a certain frustration.

As she passed her son's bedroom, she saw his tiny feet rocking his chair on the floor, his torso bent into the seat cushion. A smile crept across her lips. How could anyone sleep that way? The door still hung open from the top hinge, two screws hiding in the carpet, waiting for someone to put them back where they belonged. Bending down, she picked them up and placed them on top of the dresser. Thankfully, he unscrewed the door and not an electrical wall plate.

Crawling into bed, she curled into her pillow and away from Derek—for comfort purposes only. That's what she told herself.

The next morning, Kat cracked an eye open to find Derek gone. He never got out of bed before her. As she adjusted the old t-shirt she slept in, she stumbled down the hallway toward the kitchen. Derek stood at the counter, staring at nothing.

"What are you doing up?"

He shrugged. "Had no reason to stay in bed."

"Oh." The expression came out sounding flat. "Are you going in early?"

"I hadn't planned on it."

She brushed past him as she opened the fridge and pulled out some milk and eggs. "Breakfast?"

"Kat, are we going to pretend we didn't fight last night?"

A pan clanged on the stove as Kat put it down harder than intended.

"Couples fight, Derek, especially when things get stressful."

His hand rested near his pocket, but rose to his hip as he stepped away from the counter. "I love Joey too. He's my son. But I can't live a life where I don't get to be alone with you."

She rolled her eyes. "We can still..."

Brushing up against him, she trailed her finger down his neck until it landed on his collar.

He jerked away. "That's not what I mean and you know it."

She turned back to the stove and cracked a couple of eggs into the pan. "Mom will watch him when she visits."

"Twice a year? How is that okay with you?"

"We can travel to her. It's not super far."

"I'm not driving for over an hour when someone can watch him here."

"I told you, Derek, right now Joey needs me more. I can't leave him with...with some stranger again!"

"Nancy wasn't a stranger. She spent more than two months with him, and you spent most of the time in the other room. You loved the way she worked with him. This is ridiculous."

"Would you like some eggs?"

"Kat!"

"What? I'm not ready to trust someone else to take care of him, not yet—not now."

"So when?"

"How am I supposed to know, Derek?"

She twisted around and pointed the eggy wooden spoon at him.

"Our child got rushed to urgent care because his respite provider screwed up. How am I supposed to suddenly get over that, huh?"

"She didn't screw up. Things happen."

"You're right. She didn't screw things up. I did. I screwed up when I left him with her. The whole thing—my fault. Blame me, please, because I do. I won't leave him again. I just won't."

Kat stirred her burning eggs as Derek walked out of the kitchen toward the front door.

Going in early after all, figures.

Working Wonders

Not Now, Steve.

Derek's boss approached him from the right as Derek finished talking to the cook about a returned meal.

"Hi, Steve. What can I do for you?"

Steve nodded his balding head toward the restaurant office, and Derek dragged his feet in that direction, following his boss.

He'd come in early to get away from irrational people. As he entered the small office, Derek shut the door and stood against the wall. Steve flicked piles of paperwork with his thumb, and Derek eyed the greasy wall behind him, his eyes landing on old, stained pages tacked to the notice board.

"What's up?"

"Derek, you've worked here for several years now, haven't you?" Steve asked.

"Seven."

"And how're things going for you?"

"Fine, but we're short on servers again today. I should really—"

Steve leaned back in the chair and rocked. "Happens quite a bit, huh?"

"Yeah, recently it's been every day. I'd fire the ones causing the problem, but it's most of them."

"How do you handle it, then?"

Derek folded his arms and shifted, leaning back against the door.

"I come in and work their job and mine, then give them a warning. After three no-shows they're gone. But that doesn't do much for the ones who call in sick or have car trouble or daycare problems."

Why was Steve asking all these questions? The process wasn't new, it was corporate regs.

"Well, we'd like to add to your responsibilities."

"What? Listen, Steve, I'm already working extra shifts to help out Mike, and things are hard at home. I need less responsibility, not more."

"It's short-term. A store's being built a few miles away, and corporate feels you're the best man to get it up and running. We've hired the managers, but they need training."

"So, it's more of a transfer?"

Steve shook his head. "We need you to continue managing here while training them there. You'll spend a week there. Then you can check in with them for an hour or so a day until they're on their feet. That's it. It should take you a month or two."

The knock on the door vibrated against Derek's shoulders, and he cracked it open.

"Customer at table ten wants to see you," Susie said as she walked back to the floor.

"What about this time?"

With a hand tossed over her shoulder, she said, "When she yelled at me to get you, I didn't ask."

He shut the door.

"I don't know how I'm going to do this, Steve, but whatever. When am I over there?"

"Tuesday. And you'll have to work next weekend."

"Of course I will. When's opening?"

"Six weeks."

Great, just great!

Derek walked out of the office toward table ten. People filled the booths and tables in the dining room. He ducked out of the way as Susie rushed past with a tray full of dirty dishes and called to Emma about unhappy customers at one of her tables. Emma's section extended past her usual because Kade hadn't shown up, and her shoulders drooped lower than normal. Derek stopped her.

"You're doing great. I'll help with your tables in about ten so you can take a break."

"Thanks," she said.

Derek watched as some of the overwhelming stress fell from her eyes.

A few steps more and he arrived at table ten. An older couple scowled at him, the wife's mouth open, ready to mollify herself by administering a verbal lashing.

"Hi, my name's Derek. I'm the manager here. How can I help you?"

"Young man, I want you to fire that server." The woman pointed at Susie. "She didn't come to see us for five minutes, and it took her another ten minutes to give us our water."

"I'm sorry to hear that. As you can see—"

"That's not all," she interrupted. "Our fries were cold and limp, and when Jerry got his burger it was pink in the middle. I'm no master chef, but I know hamburger should never be pink. You're going to give us food poisoning."

Derek glued a polite but serious smile on his face. "Ma'am, I understand your concern. Did you order the burger well-done?

"No. He asked for medium."

"A medium burger will have a slightly pink center. But it's perfectly safe." He turned to the old man. "I'd be more than happy to bring you a fresh burger with no pink."

The old man shook his head.

"He'd already eaten half the burger by the time I realized your cook was trying to poison him."

"Ma'am, I assure you, he has not been poisoned. We use one hundred percent ground sirloin, which is different than your typical ground beef." His smile wavered. "I'll go ahead and remove his food from your bill. Is there anything else I can help you with?"

"No, but we will not be coming back. Horrible food and service. You need to fire that girl."

"Susie is one of my best servers, but I'll be sure to talk to her. Here are a couple of coupons for free burgers. I hope you'll change your mind about coming back."

The woman stood up and yanked her husband's arm.

"We will not be back."

Derek excused himself and nodded at Emma to take her break as he prepared to attend to her busy tables. He stopped Susie.

"Ignore those people. I'm assuming the fries were fresh?"

"Right out of the fryer."

"Ignore them. You're doing great."

She flashed a smile at him that never reached her eyes, and he hurried to take an order from the couple seated in Emma's section several minutes previous.

Two restaurants. Perfect. How would he train those people when there weren't any customers in the store during the big training week?

The phone rang as Kat handed Joey his peanut butter sandwich, cut into four squares. Running for her mobile, she pushed the talk button about the same time Joey launched his sandwich to the floor and started screaming. Peanut butter had gotten on his bandage when he picked up the first square.

"Hello." Kat rushed toward her bedroom and shut the door, trying to drown out the wailing coming from the kitchen.

"This is Richard, with Peaceful Therapies, returning a call from Kat Burns."

"Yes. Thank you for getting back to me so quickly." She hadn't expected to receive a call until Monday. "I need a new habilitation specialist for my son. And I suggest Nancy no longer be allowed to work with children."

"Obviously, something has upset you. I can send a new therapist out for an interview this afternoon. Would you mind explaining to me what happened?"

Kat slowed her pacing and eased onto the corner of her bed.

"Today? Really?"

"Yes. Most of our providers work both weekdays and weekends."

"I see." Kat gathered her thoughts, then began speaking again. "We left Joey alone with Nancy for the very first time, and his fingers got caught in a stool. He had to get x-rays and stitches in one finger."

"Was Joey left alone?"

"She says he wasn't, but I'm not convinced. I'm sorry, but I can't trust someone after something like this has happened."

"It's completely understandable. I'll forward your concerns onto the owner. She'll want to hear about it and will look into it further."

The tightness in Kat's chest relaxed. "Thank you."

"Now," Richard said, "Mandie should arrive at your house around one-thirty if that works for you?"

"It does."

"Perfect. Mandie has several years of experience. I'm sure you'll love her. Please, don't be afraid to use her for respite, and call me with any concerns you have."

"I will, thank you."

She hung up the phone and dragged her feet as she headed toward the kitchen to clean the peanut butter from Joey's bandage and figure out what to feed him next.

A couple of hours later, Kat crossed one leg over the other as she leaned her back against the bottom of the couch. She'd purchased Joey a toy tool set, hoping it would entertain him enough to keep him away from the butter knives, not to mention the now-padlocked tool box with the screwdrivers. So far, it hadn't. He was busy crying over the plastic screwdriver that wouldn't unscrew the wall plate around the light switch.

The silverware drawer currently held no silverware. Kat had moved it all to the cabinet above the stove. As long as Joey never saw her retrieve any eating utensils, the door hinges and outlet covers remained safe.

Joey ignored the doorbell, and Kat rose to meet Mandie. With luck, this specialist understood the finer points of watching a child with autism.

The door swung open, and a woman, somewhat younger than Kat in age, grinned around Kat at Joey.

"Hi, I'm Mandie." She peeked quickly at Kat who invited her into the house with a wave of her hand.

Mandie rushed to Joey, joining him on the floor. "Hi, Joey."

Joey continued to cry but shifted his body to avoid any eye contact with Mandie.

"He's a bit upset right now." Kat offered, interested in the unusual way Mandie chose to enter the house for an interview.

"Hey, Jo-Jo, do you like building stuff?" Joey scooted farther way. "I like your building toys. I have some too. Maybe I'll bring them next time. They snap and screw together. Taking them apart is even more fun."

Joey stopped crying and sat up.

"I have some popcorn in my bag. Do you like popcorn?"

He stood up and walked toward her bag. Mandie reached in, retrieved the bag of popcorn, and stepped to the table where she lined up several popped kernels. He closed his fist around a piece and pushed it into his mouth.

She turned to Kat. "Is that how he picks up most things?"

"Yeah. Is it odd?"

"Not necessarily. I'm certain his OT spends time on it, but developing a pincer grip will help him learn to use utensils the right way."

"Really?"

"Yup. That and other fine motor skills, tying shoes, writing, that kind of stuff. His OT hasn't mentioned this?"

"Leah has him pick small items up a lot but never told me why." Kat shrugged. "I knew it would help with picking stuff up but didn't realize it helped with eating."

Mandie waved away the concern. "I didn't at first either. I understand he also doesn't want to potty-train."

"Not at all. Nancy had us try without any kind of diaper for a few weeks, but it was a disaster."

"Potty training is hard. You have to figure out why he prefers messing his diaper, and then you have to figure out how to change that. There are so many possible reasons, but we'll figure it out eventually. I probably won't jump right to it because I need to develop a trusting relationship with him first."

"Of course."

How did this woman know so much? Kat had spent hour after hour on the computer and with her head in books, and she didn't know this stuff. And her entrance? Mandie waltzed into Kat's home and instead of waiting for questions, she took the interview into her own hands, almost as if Kat was the one being interviewed.

"I would love to provide hab and respite for Joey. I see that he requires help eating and bathing, so, if it works for you, I'll be here from five until seven every day."

"Um"—Kat's eyes widened at the woman's announcement—"that should work. I can set another place at the table."

"No. I'm here to work. Plan for you and your husband. I can let you know if I need anything for Joey that you don't usually have here."

Kat raised an eyebrow, and Mandie continued, "I'm sorry. Sometimes I forget myself. Please, if you prefer I do something another way—"

"No, no," Kat interrupted, "Thank you. I think this will work out perfectly. But I don't intend to use any respite care. I left Joey with his last specialist, and he ended up with stitches."

Kat peered at Joey's hand and noticed Mandie doing the same.

"I understand your concern. I can provide respite when you are home too. Maybe you would be more comfortable if Joey and I hung out in his room while you and your husband had some alone time."

Kat felt the rush of warmth enter her cheeks.

"Oh. I...I don't know. Maybe."

"Keep it in mind. I've got a client in a few minutes, but I'll be here Monday."

The door shut as Mandie left, and Kat pulled Joey onto her lap. "Hi! What's your name?"

Dream Dynamics

The drive over to the new restaurant took no more time than Derek's usual drive to work, but he wished it had taken longer. Though he'd been home all day Sunday and then again Monday evening, stress still surged through his veins Tuesday morning.

Kat had spent two days avoiding him, while he failed to make amends with her. Why couldn't she see how she'd overreacted?

Now some pushy blond lady planned to work with Joey for two hours a day after he got home from work... if he got home from work. Nancy had known to leave when he walked through the door. This woman sat next to Joey and made him scream during dinner. How was he supposed to relax through that?

Kat, of course, adored whatever-her-name-was. The evidence shone in her eyes every time the new intruder number three corrected Joey.

Slamming the car door, Derek traipsed through the empty restaurant. Even the kitchen sparkled. A man in his mid-twenties sat in the office chair, twiddling his fingers as he stared at the stark white walls. They wouldn't stay white for long.

Derek shoved his hands in his pockets. "I'm here to train Jay and Michelle. My name's Derek."

"Hi. Michelle's not here yet." The man wiped his hand down his pants and held it out to Derek, who ignored it.

"You're Jay?"

"Sure am." He dropped his hand.

"Tell me about your restaurant experience."

"I started in fast food like everyone else. Pretty quick study. Customers love me. Eventually, I worked as a server at a local restaurant down in Casa Grande before returning to fast food where I was shift manager for a couple of years."

"So you have no experience with Baja Burgers? Are you familiar with the menu?"

"I've eaten here a couple of times, but that's it."

Derek pinched the bridge of his nose. "You realize you have to learn this menu inside and out, and you better have tasted everything on it by opening."

Jay bounced on the balls of his feet. "The cooks should show up in an hour. The servers come for training shortly after. You train the whole store, right?"

Derek sighed. "Yeah. Everyone but the cooks."

A heavy-set, middle-aged woman hurried as she marched into the kitchen. "I'm sorry, I'm sorry. My kids wouldn't stop fighting, then they called me four times on the way over. It won't happen again."

"I hope not," Derek said, "since a lot of your job is handling situations where servers and cooks don't show up on time. It's important that you do. Michelle?"

"Yes, sir."

"Call me Derek." He forced a tight-lipped smile. "Okay, Michelle, what experience do you have in the restaurant business?"

"I served tables to put myself through college."

"Nothing more?"

"Not in the food industry. But I managed a small retail store for eight years."

What had Steve gotten him into? The whole situation couldn't be more ridiculous. Had he been that green when he started as manager?

"Tell me about the menu, Michelle."

"Well, I prefer the Baja Burger. I'm guessing that's a good thing since that's the restaurant's name. I don't care for the Salmon Burger, and sometimes the fries are limp."

"Strive to fix those things." Derek leaned against the wall, crossing his arms.

Michelle shook her head. "Oh no, sir...Derek. I wouldn't know how."

"It's your job to figure out how, and I want you to get in the habit of finding only good things to say about the menu items because another part of your job is selling them."

She nodded, her eyes directed toward her shoes.

"Look you guys, I know you understand this job takes work, but I'll tell you right now, it takes more than you think and definitely more than corporate ever told you. I'll get you on the right track, but you'll have to work hard." Clapping his hands and rubbing them together, he eyed the office. "Jay, you work on memorizing and learning the menu. Michelle, you're up in the office. We've got to learn scheduling and paperwork."

An hour later, Derek headed to the booth Jay had chosen as his study carrel. Michelle took right to the scheduling program and was, if nothing else, somewhat familiar with most of the paperwork. He worried less about her capabilities, as long as she showed up on time. Jay, however, made him nervous from the get-go. Fast-food shift managers basically made sure the ketchup dispenser worked right. Derek knew the job entailed more but couldn't keep his cynicism from creeping into his thoughts. He slid the menu out of Jay's view. "What toppings are on the Baja Burger?"

"Pepper Jack cheese, jalapeno, lettuce, tomato, onion, with a spicy southwest sauce."

Impressive.

"Is there mayo in the sauce?"

"Yes. We use one hundred percent mayonnaise. However, a good substitute is our barbecue sauce if mayo is a concern. It contains no mayo or other egg products."

Derek kept his face neutral, but no one had made such a good suggestion during training before. "Tell me about the veggie burger."

"The veggie burger is vegan, containing no animal products. Each veggie burger comes with tomato, lettuce, onion, and pickles. If desired, guest may add avocado for seventy-five cents more."

"And the patty?"

"The patty contains a mixture of black beans, lentils, onion, and spices."

By the time Derek had finished sampling Jay's progress, he'd determined Jay could adequately describe ten of the fifty menu items. It was a start.

He clapped a friendly hand on Jay's shoulder. "The cooks have arrived. I want you to request a menu item you memorized today and one you haven't. You eat half and give the other half to Michelle. Once you've finished, join me in the office."

The office phone rang as Derek walked back to meet the cooks, and he rerouted to answer it. "Baja Burgers, this is Derek."

"Derek, how's today gone?"

He shut the door and slumped down onto the chair. "Steve, are you trying to kill me? I might teach these two how to run this store, but this is no *easy job*. One has no managerial experience, unless you count being a shift manager at the local fast-food joint, and he has to learn the entire menu along with his actual work. The lady showed up late for her first day and hates two of our best-selling items." He shoved his hand through his hair. "Man, I have a week to get them to a point where they can function without me on-site most of the time? I need two months, not five days."

Steve chuckled lightly into the phone. "Stressed much? Go get yourself a drink and relax for a bit, Derek. These two will grow on you. How're things at home?"

"I told you Friday. It sucks. The new intruder sits at the table making Joey cry while I try to eat whatever nonperishable boxed dinner Kat remembers to throw together. If she remembers. And she's angry at me because I backed the old intruder instead of her when Joey got hurt. Not that it's any of your business."

"That's the most I've heard about your home life since you started working for me. What is the purpose of the intruders?"

Derek huffed. "They're therapists for Joey. Apparently, he has autism."

"My nephew has autism. Your kid do math? That's the genius power my nephew has. They all have one, right? Artist, math, computers, something?"

"What? No. My son's normal."

"Normal for autism?"

"Good-bye, Steve. Let's not talk like this again, okay?"

"You work for me, remember that."

"Maybe when you stop stressing me out. I'm the best you've got, and you know it. You owe me some stress-relieving leeway."

Derek hung up the phone and curled his body over the desk, his hand clasping his short hair tightly.

A knock sounded at the door before Jay walked in. "Hey boss. My brother's autistic. Doesn't like to talk, but he can drink a soda like you wouldn't believe."

Derek closed his eyes and sat silently, refusing to punch the desk with his fist.

"Jay, if you're going to eavesdrop, don't tell me you've done it."

Jay flashed a friendly smile. "Right. But you were kind of loud."

"Great." Derek slammed his open palm on the desk, no longer capable of stopping himself from hitting something. "Let's get started."

Wheeling a chair into the doorway, Jay sat in the threshold as Derek opened the scheduling program. Michelle had been instructed to watch the cooks, making sure they stayed on task through their training, and to learn as much as she could about the cooking process at the same time. The managers never helped cook, but they did need to recognize improperly prepared food.

By the end of the day, Derek's exhaustion tugged at every muscle in his body. Pushing the talk button on his steering wheel, he called home to gauge the level of Kat's fury. He wanted to go home and curl into her arms and stay there for the rest of the night. That couldn't happen—especially if she was still angry at him.

That morning, Kat woke up angry. Seething. More so than any of the last three days. She knew some of it stemmed from her dream. Whenever things became stressful between her and Derek, she dreamed about him saying he never cared for her. He always left. The dreams tormented her, and any time she went to bed frustrated and had such a dream, it set her off for most of the next day. Still, her ability to explain her rage didn't make it any easier to dismiss.

Earlier, she'd tried thinking during housework therapy, but Joey required too much attention, and she was too enraged for the single hour spent scrubbing dishes to help. She attempted to pull her thoughts other directions with movies and music, even food, but nothing worked. In some ways, her irritability seemed to grow.

She could almost concede that she'd overreacted to Joey's injury. Derek was right. She'd watched Joey push the stool several times and never worried. But when you're watching someone else's child, shouldn't you be more vigilant than the parents?

She walked into Joey's room where he sat rocking in his chair. Ruffling his hair, she bent down and kissed him before picking him up and rocking with him on her lap. Focusing on the ruminations might be more therapeutic than pushing them away.

Nancy had been wonderful with Joey, but how was Kat supposed to know she'd stayed with him the whole time? She had no proof. Maybe she should get some cameras, but that always seemed so extreme. None of it mattered now. Nancy was gone.

She leaned her head against the chair. It did matter. Kat's actions upset Derek, and he'd hurt her. When she really contemplated it, she understood that the anger she delved into recently had little to do with Nancy and everything to do with Derek. He cared more about Nancy, who he'd called intruder number three, than he did about Joey. He couldn't remember her name, but she was more important than their son? How did he justify that?

Mandie showed up as Kat stood to start dinner. Frozen pizza? No. Her body needed something fresh, and with Mandie working with Joey, she had time to make a real dinner. Simple, but fresh, nonetheless. Walking into the kitchen she pulled out a couple of chicken breasts, seasoned them, and tossed them in the oven. Then, using what fresh lettuce was available, she made a salad. As she searched for other salad ingredients, she spotted the only viable subject. The tomato had a couple of questionable spots, but she could make it work. They also had two choices of dressing: Ranch or Italian. That was enough.

While she worked, her mind slid back into the mind-numbing questions she'd encountered all day. Why did Derek defend Nancy? She sliced through the tomato with the knife and paused. A few minutes ago, she had admitted that she might have overreacted. One of the things she loved most about Derek was his fair outlook on life. He always saw both sides of the coin. Not many people could do that.

As the phone rang for the second time, Kat set aside her poor man's salad and answered it.

"Hello."

"Hi." His voice sounded tired

"Hi, babes. How's your day been?" Kat suddenly felt apologetic.

"About how I expected. Yours?"

"Depends on how you look at it, I guess. I had one of those dreams again last night."

"Dreams?" Derek asked.

"You know, where you hate me and leave."

Derek chuckled. "One of those. Well, I'll admit these last few days have had me worried."

Silence passed over the phone line for several seconds.

"Worried enough that you'd leave?" Kat bit her lip.

"Worried that you'd kick me out."

Kat's sharp inhale caught in her throat, and she coughed, then laughed as tears filled her eyes. "I would never kick you out."

He chuckled again. "Well, I'm on my way home, be there soon."

Kat hung up the phone, and cleaned up the salad mess as Mandie walked in with Joey.

"Is the kitchen free now?"

"Yup."

"Great, I want to try to get Joey to eat a little bit of fruit with dinner. Were you able to pick up those oranges and apples?

"They're in the fridge, but I've never gotten him to eat either one before."

"He probably won't eat them today, either, but I want to try."

"Sure."

Kat walked into the living room and sat on the couch. In reality, the idea of flopping on top of her bed called to her, but she wasn't ready to be so far away from Joey. She may be able to admit to overreacting, but that didn't mean her behaviors would change so easily. Mothers experienced anxiety for a reason.

It wasn't long before Derek walked in the door. Kat straightened her back and offered an apologetic smile. She hated fighting with him. He lowered his lips to hers in greeting, gave a limp wave to Mandie, and joined Kat on the couch. Wrapping his arm around her, he pulled her close. The movement brought Mandie's proposal from the other day into Kat's mind and she stiffened, causing his arm to fall back to his lap as his eyes questioned her. She offered a soft smile and leaned against his shoulder.

"When I met Mandie, she offered to watch Joey at home while we, umm..."

Warmth sprung to Kat's face, and she saw the corner of Derek's mouth start to creep up.

"What? Watch a movie?"

The warmth fully settled in Kat's cheeks, the sensation reaching into the tips of her ears, and she bit her lip. "That's probably what she meant."

Derek pulled her close again, shaking his head, a grin plastered across his face. "Wherever your mind was, I think I'd like to go there."

Kat slid across the couch and swatted at him.

"Derek!"

"What?"

"Dinner's ready, I just have to grab the chicken."

"Great! Let's eat in the bedroom."

Constructing Halloween

A few days later, Kat waited at the end of the hall for her son to appear from his room.

"Hurry, Joey, I want a picture before the bus comes."

When he didn't show up, she traipsed down the hall where he had taken off his shoes and half of his costume. Curled into a ball on the floor, he held one foot in his hand.

"Were your shoes bothering you?"

He nodded.

"Don't you want to go to your school party today?"

No answer followed.

She scooped up Joey, his construction-worker costume and shoes from the floor, then rushed into the living room.

"The party will have candy and cupcakes, and you get to be in a parade. I'll come visit. But first you need to get on the bus."

As Kat slid a sock onto the foot Joey held out to her, he yanked it away. Dropping to her knees, she turned the sock inside out. The seam at the toe had been roughly finished. No wonder he'd taken his shoes off.

"Let's try again."

Praying her ploy worked, Kat handed her son his motorcycle and watched as he spun the front wheel. With the sock inside out, she slid it onto his foot and rushed to put the shoe on.

As she finished tying the second shoe, the bus honked, and Kat helped Joey out the door. Wandering back toward the house, she kicked a piece of gravel off the sidewalk and into the yard. She hadn't gotten a picture. Luckily, she could get a few during the parade.

As time flitted away, she hurried through a quick trip to the grocery store, where she picked up one of the last bags of candy. Derek had said he'd try to get home in time for trick-or-treating, but with his crazy training schedule, they both wondered if that would happen. A box of macaroni and cheese dropped into the cart, and she determined it would have to do for the night's dinner. Joey usually ate it. That's what mattered—especially considering the preschool Halloween party, which was sure to include sugary treats.

After paying, she checked the time and drove to the school. Luckily, she'd only purchased nonperishable items. As the last car allowed into the parking lot where the kids would promenade, she hurried to the sidewalk and watched the custodian shut the gate. A tiny princess, dressed in pink and holding Ms. Perry's hand, soon strode through the cafeteria's outer double doors.

Joey's class was first. Good.

Housed at the elementary school, the preschool often participated with the older children during special-occasion activities such as the Halloween parade and the Christmas cookie decorating night. With his class leading the rest, Joey could avoid some of the noise of the older kids, and Kat might stand a chance of getting a decent picture.

Following the princess, tiny policemen, witches, and sports stars congregated in a line, each holding a loop of a bright yellow rope. No construction worker appeared. Where was Joey? Soon, the kindergarten classes funneled out the door, then first grade.

As the parade looped past her, Kat waved at Ms. Perry, trying to get her attention. The little princess stumbled to the ground and tears rolled through the pink powder on her cheeks. Of course, the teacher's attention went straight to the crying child.

Within minutes, the entire school had filed out to the parking lot, Joey nowhere in sight. Kat dashed toward the office, her heart pumping with illusions of what could have happened to her son. As she approached the doors, she tripped, her hands and knees slamming onto the concrete and warmth oozing into her cheeks. Pain soon followed, attacking her left knee more than her right.

Picking herself up, she clapped the dust off her hands and jeans, then scanned for observers. From the far lot, sounds of laughter rang in the distance. Gratitude for the separation between the parade and office flooded through her. No one had seen.

Kat hid the scratches lining her palms with her long sleeves and opened the door.

The receptionist quickly hung up the phone.

"Hi."

"Hi. I was watching the parade and didn't see my son."

The apprehension of Joey participating and Kat somehow not seeing him, pricked at her lungs, and her breathing shallowed.

"What's your son's name?"

"Joey Burns. He attends the developmental preschool."

"One sec," the receptionist said as she dialed a short extension. "Is Joey Burns with you? His mother didn't see him in the parade… Thank you. I'll send her down."

She hung up and turned back to Kat. "He stayed in the classroom. Go ahead and sign the visitor's log, and you can go see him."

Kat signed the log and, after she was handed a sticker with a giant apple that said *visitor*, strode to the nearby classroom. Why had he stayed there, anyway? The question lingered as she pulled the door open and her gaze fell to her son.

"Joey, what happened?"

"He struggled with the noise as the class sang *Wheels on the Bus*. When I got over to him, he'd already ripped off the vest and destroyed it," an unfamiliar woman said as Kat examined the damage.

One shoulder had separated completely, and the reflective fabric hung from the orange vest in long swaying strands. The cheap costume was never expected to last long, but she'd thought it would survive the day.

"We tried to get him to walk in the parade, but he refused."

Kat nodded as she realized the woman must be an aide or something. As she lifted the silver-white fabric from the neon orange, she couldn't help but groan. "Joey, didn't you like your costume?"

He stared at her, unconcerned.

The echoes of tiny footsteps shuffling along the carpet mixed with teachers' voices seconds before the door opened, and the class filed in. Ms. Perry instructed the students to move to the rug, and they filed to specific spots, no one fighting or arguing. Joey buried his head into Kat's lap as she watched.

"Joey, go sit in your spot," Kat said.

Pressure from his head pushed against her thighs.

"Come on, Joey. We're going to have cupcakes," the anonymous aide said.

He still refused to move.

As the class sat on the rug, listening to a story, Kat rubbed Joey's back. She wanted to leave, but Joey needed to stay for class, and the slightest movement caused him to clutch her tighter. It was turning into one of those days.

Class ended, and Kat stopped by the office to sign herself and Joey out. Her knee ached from her fall.

With all her desires dashed by the reality of the day, she hobbled to the car, Joey's hand in hers.

"What are we going to do about your costume?"

"It broke," Joey said with tears in his eyes.

The force of him crumbling to the asphalt caused Kat to buckle at the waist.

"You broke it. Joey, stand up."

His ball curled tighter, and Kat leaned over and picked him up, making sure to cradle his head in one arm and his feet in another. Any other way risked her knee being kicked.

"Do you want another one?" The words fell from her mouth before she had time to think, not that it mattered. All energy depleted, she'd give him practically anything if he stopped crying and allowed her a single, decent picture.

The weakness continued, and Kat soon leaned against a cart as she searched through the remnants of Halloween costumes. That any still hung on racks amazed her.

"What about this one? It has a hammer."

Joey shook his head, his eyes darkening with each suggestion.

"There are no more construction workers," she said, testing her theory.

Joey flung his head backward, his body rigid as he shrieked.

Kat buried the bridge of her nose between her thumb and forefinger as she counted to ten. She exhaled slowly then brought her head up with a snap. Their cart rolled through the store to the home improvement section. Bright orange vests bagged in tiny clear plastic packaging hung from the shelf. Medium and large—too big. She patted Joey's head, attempting to comfort him, as she hobbled to the toy department. Nothing. Her final destination had her heart leaping toward her throat. In front of her was a single, bright orange puffer vest in Joey's size. She yanked it from the rack and softly spoke to Joey about her plan. Maybe he understood some of it.

Two hours later, she hung up the phone.

"Looks like Daddy can't come trick-or-treating this year."

She sighed. She wasn't surprised, but that didn't make it any easier. Emptying the bag of candy into a big bowl, she gingerly moved to the computer where she typed: *Two pieces each makes you a peach, any more than that and you'll be saying drat.* With a chair in hand, she placed the bowl of candy outside the front door with the simple sign hanging above it. Maybe by leaving earlier in the evening she could make it back before the entire bowl was emptied into an insolent teenager's bag.

Rubbing at her knee, she called to Joey. "Are you ready?"

His eyes sparkled brighter than they had all day.

Kat stopped massaging her sore knee and asked him to stand still for a picture. As she stepped back, he held up the small hammer from the play tool set she'd bought earlier in the month. A little bit of silver duct tape on the vest with the hat from the original costume brought the outfit together. Had she considered it, she would have done that from the start. The good ideas always came late.

After snapping a couple of extra pictures, she texted one to Derek, then held her hand out to Joey. "Let's go."

Thirty minutes after starting, Kat plopped onto one of her neighbor's short retaining walls. The ache in her knee screamed at her to stop walking and go home. Neighborhood children crowded the streets with their parents as they moved in groups from one door to the next. Joey stuffed another sucker in his mouth. Kat peeked in his pumpkin.

"Time to go home," she said as she took his hand.

Though they'd been out for a decent amount of time, traveling a straight line via the sidewalk kept the distance to home short, and it wasn't long before they arrived. Derek's car sat in the driveway. In front of the door lay the empty candy bowl.

Kat pushed the door open and shut off the porch light.

"Derek?"

She limped further into the house, allowing Joey to dive into his candy. Only a dim light shone from somewhere down the hallway.

"Joey, let's show Daddy your costume."

As a piece of chocolate found its way into his mouth, Joey clutched Kat's hand, and they walked down the hall.

The master bedroom door was opened a crack. Joey pushed past Kat and ran into the room.

Derek curled on top of the bed, a soft snore rumbling past his lips as she entered behind their son.

Through the window, Kat saw the paling colors of sky, where the evening star shined toward the earth, and glanced at her husband. She wanted to wake him, but couldn't. He obviously needed sleep.

"Come on, Joey, you can show him tomorrow after he wakes up."

Once Joey fell asleep, Kat padded into her bedroom and rummaged around before changing into yoga pants. She studied her bruised knee. What it lacked in swelling, it made up for in black and blue. How she'd managed to fall in the first place still baffled her, but she shrugged it off. Somehow, Derek slept through her noise.

Not yet tired, she wandered out to the living room and flopped on the couch with the remote.

When had Derek gotten home? They'd spoken on the phone shortly before she and Joey left to go trick-or-treating. That only took forty-five minutes. Her knee couldn't handle longer. Would it really have hurt him to text and see how far down the street they'd gotten? He could have driven down the block a little bit to see if he could find them. He'd been so loving to her since their fight after Joey got hurt. But that had never been the problem.

As the TV screen brightened through a set of commercials, she picked up the remote to change the channel and jumped.

Derek chuckled.

"You snuck up on me!"

"It is Halloween, isn't it? I've lost track of time." He looked around, "Where's Joey?"

"In bed. We came in, and you were asleep."

"Keeping my head up after working two stores is becoming impossible. When I fell asleep in the office, I decided it was time to leave."

She scoffed.

He sidled up next to her on the couch. "Hey, it's all part of our newest normal, at least until the six weeks are over."

"Then what?"

"Then, we return to our new normal."

She bit her lip. New normal? The new normal where Joey has autism and therapists visit the house? Her knee bounced once, and she winced from the pain.

"How was trick-or-treating?"

"I limped my way through it, but Joey was happy most of the time."

"You limped?"

She stretched her pant leg above the knee.

Cringing, he asked, "What happened?"

"I fell at the school when I freaked out because I didn't see Joey in the parade."

"Ouch."

She rolled her eyes. "You could say that."

"So, his makeshift costume came out pretty good. Did Joey like it?"

"I think so. He'll want to show you tomorrow. He ran in tonight, but you were sleeping."

"If I get home in time, sure. I have another early morning."

Kat nodded as she sank down further into the couch.

As Kat's body fell deeper into the couch, Derek's mind reeled. She was angry again. Of course she was. What did it matter? He spent his days dealing with two different stores, neither one able to stand on its own, and nights were spent trying to recover in time for the next day. Didn't she understand that? Probably not. In her mind it was all another ploy to spend less time with Joey. She didn't have to say it, he knew it.

He ran his hand through his hair and studied her profile as she reclined on the couch watching TV. Her teeth still clung to one side of her bottom lip. With a gentle prod from him, she lifted her legs to his lap, and he trailed his fingers across her shins and down to her feet, where he massaged gently. Her response was negligible, but she didn't pull away.

Halloween at the restaurant always came with ridiculous costumes, both on the customers and the employees. When one of the cooks walked in with draped sleeves, he'd sent him home to change. At the other store, it was a busty server. Was there a Halloween dress code disclaimer in the Baja Handbook he didn't know about? Costumes weren't a problem as long as they didn't start fires or accost others with various levels of near-nudity. Susie's costume had made him laugh. A simple T-shirt with the number 3.14 on a plate. On her head, she wore a headband with fluff that looked like whipped cream.

Already two days late, he'd received a call from corporate asking for the updated employee forms. Why they had decided to update everyone's information from his store while he was in the process of training another was beyond him, but they had. So, when finished with training, he'd hurried back to his store, trying to get the paperwork finished in time to meet Kat for trick-or-treating. She was convinced they had to go early.

The second he walked in the restaurant's door, problems bombarded him. A server took off before their replacement showed up. Customers complained about other patrons' costumes. And, because he'd been at the other store and fallen behind on his work, they'd run out of ice cream.

A minute with his head on the desk proved a mistake, or a saving grace, depending on how he chose to look at it. The paperwork still had to be finished—another early morning—but it convinced him to go home.

He'd driven home opposite his usual route and scanned the block as he passed hordes of children. None of them looked like his. And he never saw Kat either. After making two passes, he gave up and parked in the driveway. At the door lay an empty bowl. He assumed it once held candy. With a glance, he decided to pick it up on his way back out to wait for Kat and Joey, but first he needed to change.

In the bedroom, he couldn't help but lie down on the bed. That was his mistake. If he'd stayed standing, his wife wouldn't be hunkered down into the couch, smoldering with inner rage.

No matter what he did, Derek messed the whole parenting thing up. And Kat always recognized it.

Thankfully, this time, she wasn't bringing it to his attention.

He rubbed deeper into her arches.

"Does your knee hurt much?"

"Yeah."

She didn't look at him.

"Do you need to see a doctor?"

"No. It's just tender and bruised."

"Kat?"

She turned, meeting his eyes, the blue of hers lit by the light from the TV.

"I wanted to be here tonight."

"Hmm."

Excuses would get him nowhere. He had to figure out how to make her happy—convince her that he loved Joey. With everything going on, how? His jaw tightened.

Sweet Training

With all the craziness in their lives, Kat and Derek spent most days saying goodnight and good morning, hello and goodbye, without much conversation in between. Since Halloween, Derek mentioned the newest or new normal several times, but Kat had no idea how to fix either one. Still, as time wore on, she realized they couldn't spend years waiting for Joey to need less of her. The fix: Derek had to accept Joey. The question of how to make that happen continued to linger in her mind. One thing was for certain though, she wouldn't take Mandie up on her continuous offer, even if she did mean *to watch a movie.*

Derek spent so much time at work that visiting him could be a possibility. During off-hours? Maybe? He'd mentioned his schedule between the two stores, and she thought she remembered him saying he only spent an hour a day at the new one. Deciding to chance it, she loaded Joey into the car after the lunch-rush hours and set off to surprise Derek. This way they could spend time together.

As the door swung open, she shuffled into the restaurant and allowed the hostess to seat her and Joey. Kat immediately placed sugar packets in front of her son, along with the kids' menu and two crayons. He reached for the sugar packets, lining them up. Sugar couldn't hurt anything, and cleaning it up was easy enough. The plan to talk to the server about seeing Derek died when he walked onto the floor in a huff.

Exchanging words with one of the employees, he rushed over to a table and spoke with the customer, then removed a full plate of food. He smiled a tight smile and hurried back into the kitchen. A split second later, he stepped back onto the floor and to another table where he took an order.

As Kat debated whether or not to stay, Derek glanced in their direction and a happy recognition crossed his face.

After entering the kitchen one more time, he returned to the floor and slipped into a chair next to Joey.

"Hey, buddy. Are you having a good day?" He ruffled his son's hair.

Joey took another sugar packet and added it to his line.

"I didn't know you were coming in." Derek grinned at Kat.

She missed his smile more than she'd realized.

"Well, you're right. We don't see enough of each other. So, here we are. How busy are you?"

Derek's lips tightened, but still turned up at the corners.

"I shouldn't be busy at all, but two of our servers didn't show up again."

The volume of the music shot up, and Joey covered his ears and screamed. Kat lunged toward him to help cover his ears and apply some deep pressure. Derek jumped up and ran into the back. The music volume decreased again in seconds, and Derek returned.

"They're not supposed to touch the volume."

Kat mumbled as she settled back into her chair.

"I put an order of fries in for Joey. Do you want anything?"

"A milkshake. Chocolate."

Derek tilted his head. "As if I thought you'd want vanilla."

He waved down Susie and told her to bring a milkshake out when she had a chance. He emphasized the no rush part.

Conversation flowed easily. He had to go to the other restaurant in about an hour. The progress the managers had made pleased him, but he also told her he had plenty more to do. She understood his concern, though she didn't understand everything he said.

"Are their servers showing up?"

"Yes, but their servers are also getting fed every day as they learn the menu and still have no one to actually serve. Give them a couple of months and they'll have similar problems to the ones we have here."

"Why you?"

Derek shrugged. "I'm the best."

Kat giggled, but stopped short as his demeanor changed. "I'm sorry. I know they depend on you."

The milkshake arrived, and with it an overwhelmed Susie. "Derek, I can't take care of all these tables."

"Give me one more minute," he said.

The overworked girl left, her feet hitting the floor with heavy steps. Kat opened her mouth, ready to tell Derek to leave, when sugar exploded into the air, striking her in the face. Joey screamed.

Derek stood. "I have to go."

Kat nodded, and worked to calm Joey down, frustrated Derek couldn't stay.

"Maybe we can come with you to the other store?"

She scooped part of her milkshake into a spoon and offered it to Joey, wishing he would stop wailing.

"I don't know, Kat. I have a lot to do, and I can't worry about you guys."

"I know. I'll take care of Joey. The car ride alone is ten more minutes with you."

"Let me think about it."

Derek rushed into the office. Leaving two servers alone for the entire restaurant would not bode well.

After spending half an hour on the phone trying to find someone to come in, he gave up and called Michelle at the other location.

"I need you to send two servers over to my store."

"I don't think that's a good idea. They still need training."

"And I'm in charge of that training, so I get what they need. Send me Ana and Grace. They have experience and know most of what's on the menu. Facing real life will be good for them."

He raked his hand through his hair as he listened to Michelle voice her concerns, but then a shriek rang through the restaurant, and Joey burst into the kitchen.

"Michelle, I have to go. Send them over."

Jumping from his chair, he scooped Joey into his arms and met Kat as she rushed in after their son.

"What's going on?" he asked, exasperated.

"I'm sorry. I don't know. He dumped his fries on the floor, and when I started cleaning them up, he took off."

"He can't be doing that here, Kat. If we'd been busy someone could have gotten hurt." Derek's pulse raced as he developed a tic in his left index finger. "I think you guys better go home."

Kat took Joey from Derek, and a tear escaped her eye. "I only wanted to spend time with you."

"I know, but work probably isn't the best place. Maybe Mindi—"

"Mandie."

"Why don't you ask Mandie to stay late one night this week. If you don't want to go out, we can hang out at home."

"Just us again?"

"Yes, just us."

Kat's eyes darkened, and she glared at Derek with disbelief and anger. "What's your problem? Why don't you want to spend time with Joey?"

"What are you talking about? Of course I want to spend time with him!"

"But you don't. You don't spend time with him, and when you talk about spending time with anyone, it's always without Joey."

"Kat, I don't have time for this." His hand crushed his short hair. "I want to spend time alone with you because you're my wife. That doesn't mean I don't want to spend time with Joey or that I don't love him."

"Really? The last time we did anything as a family was that baseball game you dragged us to. Remember how that turned out?"

Derek seized Kat's hand and dragged her into the office where the kitchen staff didn't have such great seats to the circus.

"I thought we were over that."

Kat turned away from Derek and let Joey slip to the floor before both of her arms flew into the air, a show of resignation. "We were, we are."

"Are we?"

"Look, ever since Joey was diagnosed, you've treated him differently."

"Me? I don't think so Kat. You're the one who's changed. You baby him and won't leave his side. If he starts crying you run over to help him stop—"

"He's three!"

"He needs to learn how to function."

"That's why he has therapists, Derek!" She spat his name out as she glowered at him. "I'm doing the best I can. Until I knew what was wrong, I had no idea how to parent my child. Now that I do, I intend to give him the very best care."

Derek put his hand on her shoulder, but she shook it off.

"I want what's best for him too, Kat, but that doesn't mean we put every little thing he needs ahead of our own needs."

"Yes, Derek, right now, it does. He's our baby. We're the adults."

He swallowed deeply. "We are. And I'll work on spending more time with both of you, but do you think you and I could spend some time alone too?"

"I'll think about talking to Mandie." Her voice softened. "But the idea of someone hanging out in our house with Joey while we're in another room alone..."

Her words fell away.

"Is weird?" Derek raised a single eyebrow as Kat realized what she was saying.

"Yeah, almost like there's an intruder in our home."

Derek chuckled and leaned over, gently kissing Kat, then picked up Joey, swinging him up to his shoulders. "Come on, I'll walk you out to the car. Why don't you pick a movie the three of us can watch together tonight?"

The rest of the afternoon and evening yanked Derek's nerves into a tightly-bound mess. Ana and Grace arrived at one restaurant as he left for the other, then halfway through the training, he received a call from Susie.

"You need to come back."

Derek's brow knit together. He had servers who couldn't remember the menu, let alone carry a tray. "That's a little hard right now. What's going on?"

"These girls you sent over... You said they had experience."

"Ana and Grace are better than the other choices I had to offer."

"Well," Susie said, exasperation leaking into his ear, "Grace keeps giving customers the wrong orders, and Ana has dropped two trays. Luckily, they were empty."

Derek closed his eyes as he leaned against the desk. "Their store opens in three weeks. Tell them to slow down and try to relax."

"I'd love to, but we're packed right now. People have already complained about us taking too long."

How on earth was he supposed to handle this situation?

"I'll be right there. Looks like training's at our location tonight."

Walking back to the group of lightly trained servers, Derek clapped his hands. "I've got a surprise for everyone. Pack up your stuff, we're going to the

Deer Valley store and working tables with customers for the next two hours."

Color drained from their faces as they turned to each other for support.

Michelle's eyes widened, and she rushed to Derek. "What are you doing?"

"Look, I'm in charge of two stores at the same time. The Deer Valley location is short-staffed, and these guys need experience."

"You've been watching them, right?"

"Yeah. Well, I have you and Jay to back me up."

"What?"

Derek waved Jay over. "Jay, once we're there, you'll be in charge of the kitchen staff. Keep them on target, and keep everything flowing in there. That includes answering the phone and making sure the cooks have everything they need to do their jobs." He turned to Michelle. "You're going to be with me, helping the servers and checking with customers. You'll take the front; I'll take the rear." He scanned from Michelle to Jay and back as he said, "You guys, if either of you run into something you aren't sure of, come find me."

The idea of putting this untrained staff on the floor of his restaurant caused Derek's shoulders to tighten. The base of his head ached. Steve would never hear the end of this—not from Derek. His finger tapped at his belt.

Jumping out of the car after the ten-minute drive, he dashed into the back of the store and told his staff what to expect. After counting the extra servers, he peered at the floor gathering his thoughts.

"We're in a decent position here tonight, everyone. Susie and Emma can handle their normal sections. The rest of you will double up and share. Work together. Be prompt, but don't rush. If you have any kind of a problem, Michelle will be up front and I will be in the back. We only have two hours left on our shifts. This is a great way to learn what you still need to work on. Michelle, assign them their sections."

Michelle nodded and turned to the group. Derek left to find his overwhelmed servers. Susie glanced at him as he walked onto the floor and rushed over.

"Don't ever do that to me again," she said.

He put his hand on her shoulder. "Sorry, Sus. You're the best I've got. You know that, right? I brought all the trainees."

"You did what?"

"They're doubling up on sections. I'll be here. You don't need to worry about it. You and Emma take your normal sections, and try to relax."

"Right," she said as she strode off.

He owed her more than he could give and made a note to call Steve and tell him to figure out some way to recognize both Susie and Emma.

It took a bit for everyone to get the flow of what was going on. Jay needed some help in the kitchen, and a few servers upset customers, but in the end, Derek found training the group with real customers boosted their spirits and forced them to remember what they'd learned.

By the end of the shift, he'd decided to continue training them in his store during his time with them. Michelle and Jay could handle the rest. Why the entire staff consisted of people with no Baja Burger experience still confused him, but he could see a way to handle it now.

The drive home helped him relax, but he struggled with the idea of trying to watch a movie with the possibility of Joey melting down. Still, Kat was right. He needed to spend time with his son. He did love him, but maybe he hadn't shown it very well recently.

As the front door swung open, the aroma of fresh popcorn welcomed him. Better yet, Kat met him in the living room and offered a warm kiss. He'd missed the softness of her lips more than he'd realized.

"Hi. Where's Joey?"

"In his room, rocking."

"With intruder number three?" *Of course.*

"I sent Mandie home a bit early. Tonight, it's just us."

He ran his hands down her arms and lured her closer. "Don't toy with me."

"I'm not."

With more force than before, he held Kat in his arms, his lips pressed against hers. This time, he took the time to explore them, tasting the salt from a stolen piece of popcorn. His heartbeat rose as he drew her closer, his arms ensconcing her body. As he loosened his grip, Kat dropped from her tiptoes back to the floor, her chest rising and falling in rhythm with his.

"Um," she said, flustered, "I've got popcorn and M&M's r-ready in the kitchen."

"I'll get Joey," he said, a lighter bounce in his step.

Derek found Joey rocking in his chair and spinning the front wheel on a blue motorcycle. "Hey, buddy, is that a new motorcycle?"

Joey didn't answer but climbed out of the chair and walked toward Derek, who pointed at the motorcycle. "Is that a new motorcycle?"

"No. A bike."

"A bike, huh? What do you think about watching a movie and eating some popcorn with me and Mama? What movie should we watch?"

Joey didn't answer but took Derek's hand, and they walked into the living room together. Kat had several movies laid out for them to choose from. And as Derek studied the options, Joey wandered toward the closed movie cabinet. "Joey wants Baby."

"What, buddy?" Derek glanced at Kat.

"*Jumbo*. He calls it *Baby*. It's his favorite."

Jumbo, Derek mouthed, his eyes meeting Kat's from under a raised brow. She nodded. He shook his head as Kat tilted hers, beaming.

"How about we choose one from over here, Joey." She took his hand and brought him back to the movies she'd laid out.

Joey pulled toward the cabinet again. Derek waited, his nerves bracing for a meltdown. It never came.

"Joey, these are the movies you can watch tonight. Not *Baby*. Which one would you like?"

"Joey wants *Baby*."

"We can watch *Baby* tomorrow," she said. "Tonight we can watch one of these. Do you like Dragons?"

Joey shook his head.

"I like *Cars*," Derek offered. He picked up the box and showed it to Joey. "See, there's Mater. Do you want to watch Mater?"

Joey glanced at the case with Mater and Lightning McQueen on the front, then to the closed cabinet. He ran to the couch and sat down. Derek gave Kat a look. Did that just happen? Had Joey given in?

"How?"

"A lot of work. A lot. And plenty of meltdowns, but he's had a restful afternoon. You know, after he fell apart at the restaurant. It makes it easier." She grinned.

"Well, I'm not arguing or wasting time."

After sliding the movie into the player, he curled his arm around Kat and rubbed Joey's head.

"No, Daddy." Joey pushed Derek's hand away.

"Sorry, buddy."

Shortly into the movie, Kat nudged Derek and nodded in Joey's direction. Looking past Kat, he saw Joey's head resting on his tiny chest, which rose and fell in an even rhythm. Derek shifted away from Kat, took two steps, and leaned over, picking Joey up.

In Joey's room, He laid his sleeping son in the rocking chair. Joey's eyes fluttered before he started rocking back and forth.

Derek leaned against the wall, the hallway light faintly illuminating the room. How could anyone think he didn't love this sweet boy? He was a handful, but he held Derek's heart too. The meltdowns shouldn't bother him like they did. They were embarrassing though. Something had to change. Derek had to change. But how? He wanted nothing more than to

157

raise a family, but wants weren't abilities, and clearly, he had none of those.

Kat's arms folded around Derek's waist from behind, capturing his attention, and he brought her to his side.

"I'm sorry," he said.

"For what?"

"For letting his meltdowns get to me."

A twinkle shone in Kat's eyes. "They get to me too."

He lowered his lips to hers, and they walked out of the room. As Kat started back to the living room, he tugged her toward him. With his arms wrapped around her, he lowered his head close enough to feel her sweet breath caress his chin. "This way."

The bedroom door swung open.

Cherry on Top

"Are you coming today?"

"Coming where?" Kat asked Derek as her head poked through the top of her chosen t-shirt.

"The new restaurant opens today. I thought you might bring Joey by for an ice cream."

Dropping the readied ponytail she held in her hand, Kat stared at her husband. "Do you think that's a good idea? You do remember what happened a few weeks ago, right?"

After a wonderful night watching *Cars* as a family, Kat went out of her way to show Derek attention. She recognized his attempt to include Joey by inviting him to the opening, but the idea of Joey in a noisy restaurant packed with people caused her insides to tremble.

"Yeah, but you don't have to stay long, and you can sit in the office where it's quieter."

"In the office?"

Derek chuckled. "Michelle keeps this office clean, much better than I keep mine."

"What time are you thinking?"

"Half hour before open, about ten-thirty. Then I can introduce you to a few people."

"You mean you've made friends?"

"Might not call them friends, but people, you know."

"Okay, but I don't want to get in your way."

"I'm there more for support. It'll be fine."

Derek goosed her behind and strolled out of the bedroom.

"Wait. Are you leaving now?"

He stood waiting by the front door as she turned the corner.

"Being on time might be a good idea," he said.

"Well, I like good-bye kisses."

"I gave you a squeeze."

She rolled her eyes and lifted herself onto her tiptoes. He pecked her lips as she leaned in.

"Wait. That wasn't a kiss. I'm not following you today."

But Kat knew his game, and she did follow him. She followed him straight to the car where he rolled down his window and allowed her one, slightly more personal kiss.

"Goodbye," she whispered.

"See you in a couple of hours."

Back inside, Kat cleaned a few dishes left in the sink and began picking up the blocks Joey had lined up in front of the couch. If she didn't put them away before he woke, she'd never get the chance. Of course, in all likelihood, they'd be back in a line by the time they left for the restaurant. Still, if she took care of them now, she could vacuum. The scattered crumbs and tiny pieces of debris made vacuuming a necessity.

Leaning over for the last block, Kat spotted her son hauling blocks out of their case. She pushed her hair behind her ear with a huff. When did he get up?

"Joey, let's get you breakfast."

"No. Joey want blocks."

"After breakfast."

She took his hand in hers, but he yanked it away. As she snapped the lid on the case, he collapsed to the floor and banged his head on the carpet. After placing the case on top of a high shelf, she grabbed the vacuum. Breakfast was on hold until he told her what he wanted anyway.

The sound of the vacuum filled the room as Joey's screams worked to match it. Kat ignored the screaming and head banging as much as possible, but when a large clatter sounded behind her, that ended.

An entire shelf of children's books and two more shelves of toys lay strewn across the floor behind her. Joey perched himself on the third shelf, clinging to the fourth. Never before had Kat been so thankful for her insistence that the shelves be fastened to the wall.

"Joey, get down."

"Joey want blocks."

"No blocks. It's time for breakfast."

Joey stared at Kat then reached for the blocks on the now top-heavy fifth shelf, his foot maneuvering as he prepared to climb higher yet again.

Kat snatched him from the shelf and sat him on the couch. "No. Stay here."

Another meltdown ensued, and Kat removed the case of blocks from the shelf, ready to hide them in a closet, but her grip relaxed. If she hid the blocks, her entire day promised nothing but meltdown after meltdown. The idea of having another day like that, after having him fall apart over every little thing yesterday, exhausted her. Add Derek's invitation, request really, that they visit the restaurant, and Joey soon found himself in possession of a case full of blocks, while Kat sorted through the pile of books and toys on the floor. From now on, she'd pick up the blocks before going to bed. One more demanding thing to add to her motherhood schedule.

With the blocks lined up again, Joey settled down for breakfast and ate the toast Kat had finally learned how to make. Deciphering the wants of such a particular three-year-old never got easier, but he was consistent.

A cup of coffee later, and Kat rubbed the head of the boy who wanted nothing more than his mother's attention.

"Should we play a game?"

Joey crawled onto Kat's lap as she sat on the couch.

"What should we play?"

She sang the beginning of *Itsy-bitsy Spider*, but Joey placed his hand over her mouth.

"No *spider*, huh? *Wheels on the Bus?*"

He shook his head.

"Okay George, what do you want to play?"

A smile broke across his face. "I not George."

"You're not? Then who are you? I know, you're Timothy."

"I not Timoffy."

Kat put a finger to her mouth. "Hmm. I know, you're Jesse!"

"I not Jesse." He giggled, putting his face closer to hers, waiting.

"Well, then you must be David!"

"I not David. I Joey!"

Kat brought her son into a huge hug, then tickled him to the soft cushions on the couch. "You're not Joey. You're David."

"I not David. I Joey." The words left his mouth between giggles. "Mama, I Joey!"

"Okay, you're Joey. I love you, Joey."

Kat held Joey against her side, wrapping her left arm tightly around him.

That silly game had become so much more than a tool to teach him his name. They both loved it. It was during those sparse, playful times that she knew her son loved her as much as she loved him.

"Joey, do you want to go see Daddy?"

His eyes opened wider, a gleam shining within each one.

"Go get your shoes. Daddy says you can have ice cream."

"Joey want ice cream."

"K—go get your shoes."

He climbed off the couch and headed to the hall closet where they kept the shoes. Kat watched. Most of the time, Joey refused to get his shoes. Opening the door, he peered at the footwear on the floor. His little body crumpled to the carpet as he kicked at the door. He'd opened the door—it was something.

She walked over. Leah had mentioned that struggling to find an item in a pile of disarray could overwhelm Joey. Kat figured a pile of shoes in the closet qualified. Still, he'd tried.

"Let's see. Look Joey, there're your shoes."

She pointed at the footwear, hoping he'd follow her finger. Nope. She bent down and picked up the sneakers and Joey. Once he saw them in her hand, he calmed down. Apparently, he really wanted ice cream.

The time in the car passed quickly, and Kat soon found herself knocking on the door of the newest Baja Burger. No one answered.

Digging her phone out of her purse, she texted Derek: *We're here.*

It didn't take long before the door swung open, and Derek met her with a kiss on the cheek. "You made it."

"Barely. This morning has not been easy."

"Hey, buddy, do you want some French fries?"

Joey whined.

"I think he wants ice cream, Daddy," Kat said, throwing Derek an exasperated look. "That's what you offered earlier."

"Ice cream! Is that what you want, Joey?"

Joey nodded his head as he spun the front wheel on his newest motorcycle.

"Then that's what you'll get. Chocolate or vanilla?

No answer.

"He usually eats vanilla," Kat said.

Derek nodded in response. "I want you to meet Michelle and Jay."

Kat followed Derek toward the kitchen. He'd mentioned Michelle several times recently, and she got the impression he relied on her more than Jay.

A heavy-set woman, wearing a manager's shirt, stepped out of the kitchen to speak with one of the servers. The server listened to what she had to say and changed direction.

"Michelle," Derek called out.

The woman stopped.

"I'd like you to meet my wife, Kat, and our son, Joey."

"Derek mentioned you were coming by today." The woman grinned at Kat as she shook her hand. "I'm certain you'll be happy to have him home more. Give or take a week."

"I don't plan on being here past this week."

"We'll see about that, boss." She raised an eyebrow and smiled. "I need to go check with the cooks, make sure they're ready. Less than twenty minutes, now."

Michelle excused herself, and Derek led Kat into the kitchen where she met a few servers as they passed them on their way to the floor.

In the office, he had two small chairs pulled up to a spotless desk. "I put everything out of this little guy's reach."

"I wish I'd done that at home."

165

Derek's confused look reminded her that he had no clue what she was talking about. She shook her head at the memory of the mess of books and toys.

"He climbed the shelves and knocked all the books and a bunch of toys down."

Derek's grimace said everything she needed to hear.

Joey squirmed, and Derek lowered him to the floor.

"Derek," Kat said, before the *oh-crap* look crossed his face.

Joey ran out of the office toward the kitchen. Jumping out of his seat, Derek flew after him and almost knocked down a startled guy, also wearing a manager's uniform. Kat guessed he was Jay.

"Hey, Der—"

"Hang on, sorry," Derek said, swooping down and catching Joey as he ran toward the kitchen staff. "Oh no you don't. Where do you think you're going?"

Joey's scream echoed through the kitchen as he flung his head into his father's chin. Derek's face turned bright red. Kat, who'd dashed out of the office about as fast as her husband, mouthed the words *ice cream.*

Her heart beat in her chest, praying Derek wasn't too upset. They never should have entered the office without giving Joey his ice cream. How had her thoughts gotten away from her? Meeting Derek halfway, she took Joey in her arms and told him Daddy would get his ice cream. The screaming continued.

"Boss?"

"Hey, yeah." Derek clenched his jaw.

"Hey, I—"

"Spit it out, Jay."

"Sorry. You want me in here, right?"

Derek closed his eyes and pinched the bridge of his nose. Kat saw the exasperation written on his face.

"You and Michelle were deciding who was where, remember? What're you going to do tomorrow when you're the only one here?"

"That's tomorrow." Jay shrugged. "I need to know about now."

"Go talk to Michelle. I'm only here for major fallout."

"Right."

Derek turned back to Kat as she struggled with Joey. "Ice cream. Got it."

She watched as he rushed toward the soft-serve ice cream machine and swirled the perfect pile of vanilla into a bowl. After grabbing a spoon, he ushered them back into the office.

Joey glared at the bowl of ice cream as Derek set it in front of him then flung it away.

"What's wrong now?" Anger flashed in Derek's eyes.

Kat shook her head. "I have no idea. Maybe we should leave."

"No. I'll get him some chocolate."

"Derek, I don't know—"

He left the office before Kat finished.

She leaned over and collected her son off the floor. "Daddy's going to bring you chocolate ice cream, okay?"

Did it matter?

"Here you go. I put a cherry on top for you too," Derek said to their son as he entered the room with a tight smile plastered on his face.

They were nothing more than customers now.

Joey reached for the ice cream, but Kat pushed it back before it ended up on the floor. "He doesn't like cherries. I think we better go."

"No. If I can't get an order right for my own son, I don't belong in this business."

He raked his hand through his hair, and Kat saw the muscles in his jaw tighten.

She removed the cherry from the top and slowly scooted the ice cream toward Joey. He picked up the spoon and pitched it across the room. Derek's tightened face turned red, anger cascading in ripples through his muscles.

"We need to go. Thank you for inviting us, but you're busy."

Derek nodded, saying nothing.

Carrying a wailing Joey in her arms, Kat shuffled out of the kitchen before rushing to the parking lot. Tears streamed down her face. He'd tried so hard, but embarrassment still forced its hand. She'd tried to tell him. Bringing Joey never turned out right. It always made him angry. All she wanted was a normal family. But they weren't normal. Joey had autism, and that ruined Derek's life.

Embarrassing Escapades

Derek slammed his fist down on the office desk and lowered himself into a chair, then quickly stood again. The ice cream spattered across the desk as he grabbed it and headed into the kitchen. There was no way he could sit in the office all day. His foot caught a loose piece of lettuce, and he slid two feet forward before finally catching his balance.

"Clean this mess up before someone kills themselves!"

Silence overtook the kitchen, every eye turning to him before a line cook rushed to grab a broom.

The bowls of uneaten ice cream clinked in the sink, and Derek stalked toward the floor almost running over a server on his way out. "Remember to yell *blind*! Can't anyone do anything right?"

Customers filled the tables, and the servers hurried from one table to another, each one looking harried. Derek spotted Michelle as she dealt with a customer. Neither looked happy.

"Sir, I need to ask you to leave now," Michelle said.

Derek trod to the table. "Is there a problem here?"

"No," Michelle said, her gaze never leaving the customer. "This gentleman was just getting ready to leave."

Derek put his hand on Michelle's shoulder, but she refused to turn away from the customer.

"Michelle."

"Are you her boss?"

Derek met the customer's eye.

"I was minding my own business and she comes up and starts telling me I have to leave because some pretty little waitress doesn't like me."

"I'm sorry for any confusion, sir. May I please speak to you, Michelle?"

"In a minute," she said, never removing her eyes from the customer. "If you don't leave, I'll ask my associate to call the police."

"I'm sure that won't be necessary, Michelle," Derek said with hooded eyes.

The man shoved his plate away. "This food isn't worth my money anyway."

Several other customers gawked at the escalating situation, turning and whispering to each other as the man stomped off.

Derek turned to Michelle, "Go to the office, now."

Pushing a hand through his hair, he put on a smile and stepped from table to table, offering an apology and a small discount for those who witnessed the ordeal. As he approached one table, a middle-aged woman spoke before he had the chance.

"You have no idea what happened. That man slapped a young lady's behind, and you apologized to him, didn't you? Did you even stop to think about that before you got mad at the other gal? She handled the situation right. Didn't need any help from you."

A knot formed in Derek's stomach, and his eyes dropped to the edge of the table momentarily before rising to meet the woman's.

"I was unaware of all of the circumstances. A small discount will be provided for your meals." He bowed his head again. "If you'll excuse me, I need to apologize to my co-worker."

How could he let so much anger control him? Michelle handled the situation like a saint, and he'd chastised her. As common sense returned, he realized he owed several staff members apologies. Inside the kitchen, he rubbed his hands down his face, taking a beat to collect his thoughts.

Before meeting Michelle, he called for attention in the kitchen. "I've allowed my personal life to get in the way and took my anger out on you guys. You're doing a great job, and I'm sorry."

Comments rumbled through the line as the cooks returned to their work.

Derek trod to the office, seeing Michelle bristle in her seat.

"You don't even know what—"

He held his hand up, quieting Michelle.

"A customer already explained what a louse I am. I'm sorry for the way I treated you."

Michelle sat back in her chair with a grunt.

"Which server was it?"

"Grace."

"Is she okay?"

"I don't know. She couldn't stop shaking, so I sent her home."

"The police should have been called."

"Yes." Agitation colored her voice again. "They should have, but I couldn't leave, and when I sent Leslie to find you, you screamed at her for not calling *blind*."

"What?" Derek sank into a chair. "I-I've lost it. I've completely lost it," he muttered under his breath. "Where is she? I need to apologize. Crap, I can't believe I did this to you guys."

"Yeah. You let the innocent actions of your little boy embarrass you so much that you lashed out at all the other faultless people around you. Why?" Michelle scowled at him, waiting for an answer.

"I can't help being embarrassed."

"Yes you can, but if you won't, then you should at least learn to control your frustrations around others."

Derek didn't want to get into a conversation like this. He'd screwed up enough.

"Look, tell me where Leslie is, and get me Grace's number. Did that idiot pay at all? We could pull info from his charge."

"No, he didn't. Leslie's working section four."

Derek placed his hand on Michelle's shoulder. "Thanks."

He meant it. How had he managed to let so much anger build up over something so small? Autism or not, three-year-olds were notorious for crying for what they wanted and running away from their parents. Still, he didn't understand how Joey had gotten past him and Kat, not to mention Jay. He exhaled sharply. Jay wouldn't have known to grab Joey, but he and Kat did. Derek grumbled to himself, trying not to let his thoughts take over.

Leslie stood at a table taking an order. He approached as she finished and asked if they could speak. Her body stiffened as he led her to the edge of the room out of others' way.

"Listen, Leslie, I never should have yelled at you like that. I didn't call out either. Moreover, you were coming to find me under miserable conditions, and I never gave you the chance to talk."

She raised her chin, still struggling to meet his eyes. "I still screwed up. I didn't call out, and I didn't call the police."

Tears streamed down her reddened cheeks.

He scuffed the floor with his foot. He'd made servers cry before, but not under these circumstances.

"You did exactly what you needed to. I'm sure there's a billion other ways we could have handled that jerk, but we can't turn the clock back now. Let's move forward. I'm proud of you and the job you're doing here."

"Thank you." She sniffed and wiped at her eyes.

"Okay then"—he scanned the room—"why don't you go relax in the office for a bit. I'll take care of your section until you feel like you can return."

She wiped her eyes again, and he heard her call out *blind* as she passed through the doors on the way to the office.

Derek picked up an order, carrying the tray to one of Leslie's tables, when Steve walked in. Smiling at the customers, Derek delivered the food and checked on the next table as he watched Steve enter the kitchen. By the time he'd checked with the next table, Leslie had returned to the floor.

Without exchanging words, Derek went to the office where Steve waited for him. Why did he have to deal with him today?

"Steve."

"Derek."

Steve held out his hand, and Derek grasped it begrudgingly.

"Why are you here?"

"I thought I'd stop by and see how things are going. Other than finding you waiting tables while a server sat in the office, everything seems like it's going well."

"Leslie was in the office because a customer got fresh with her co-worker. When she came to get me, I yelled at her for not remembering to call out."

Steve chuckled. "Well, she did need to do that."

"I think we can forgive her this time." Derek's derision shined through, but Steve seemed to ignore it.

"Derek, you look worn out. I'm here to tell you you're getting an award and a promotion, if you accept it."

Derek couldn't help but laugh at the irony. "For what?"

"For what? For this." Steve waved his arm above his head. "You've taken a pile of people with no experience and turned them into a miracle. The store opened on time. Six weeks. That's unheard of. No one believed me when I said you could do it, but I knew you could. This award... it's a big deal. It'll be given at the Baja Holiday Picnic, so you and your wife better be there."

Derek nodded, unable to speak. He'd never expected an award. He hadn't expected anything more than a headache.

"You did hear me mention a promotion, right?" Steve eyed him curiously.

"Yeah...yeah, what was is it?"

"A new position. We have more stores than we can handle right now. That's why you were asked to train this one. We want you as our first operations director. It means a lot of traveling, training new stores, and you may want to move. But the money? A salary increase of forty percent."

"Why would I move?"

"Most of the stores are in Tucson. You know that."

Tucson. "Right. I guess moving would make sense. I'll need to talk to my wife; you know how it is."

"Sure do." Steve stood up. "Talk to Kat, and don't miss the picnic. It's next week, remember." He stopped at the door and pointed at Derek before leaving. "You and your wife. Your son's welcome too. Kids love picnics, and they have a train ride there. I think a Santa Claus is scheduled too."

"Maybe." After the day he'd had, taking Joey anywhere felt more like a train wreck than a fun ride.

Derek had two more people he needed to apologize to that day, and the prospect sobered him on his drive home. He did need to learn to control his emotions when it came to Joey. Stupid meltdowns—autism—whatever it was. How did other guys do it? He huffed. Maybe parenting wasn't for him. He certainly sucked at it recently.

People pretended like they never noticed when Joey fell apart. But Derek's skin burned under their gawking stares, and he heard their muttered comments about someone needing to control their child. How Kat ignored them, he had no idea. She probably never noticed. The screaming bit into his eardrums, ringing uncomfortably in his head every time. Letting it go for a time at home, he could handle, but more than once, he'd come unglued in public. Kat kept telling him he needed to relax and accept it as a part of life. As if it was that easy.

He turned onto his street and tried to set the thoughts aside, but one more snuck through: *maybe Joey would be better off without me.*

Settled in the driveway, he placed his head on the steering wheel, preparing himself to meet his angry wife. How could she not be angry? This time his actions made *him* angry. Exhaling, he stepped out of the car and walked into the house. Kat met him at the door, and Joey bounced on his toes asking to be picked up.

"Hi?"

"You say that like you're surprised." Kat pecked him on the cheek.

He picked up Joey, squeezing him until he wiggled to get down. "I figured I'd be facing a firing squad."

"A firing squad? For what?"

He shrugged. "Putting a cherry on top of ice cream. I don't know."

Kat led Derek to the couch and helped Joey onto her lap, where he sat spinning the wheel of his motorcycle.

"Look, I told you about my morning with Joey. I knew what to expect. Avoiding a meltdown would have been like lying in a box of rattlesnakes and expecting to not be bitten. Didn't you expect that?"

"I never know what to expect."

"Crowds, noise, and food are his biggest triggers. After that comes clothing, inconsistency, and whatever else happens to get on his nerves that day."

"But you're not mad?"

"What exactly did you do to make you think I'd be mad?"

"I got mad."

Kat smiled. How did she smile?

"Yeah, you didn't hide that very well, but Joey didn't know you were upset, and I doubt any of your employees did either. A clenched jaw is nothing like yelling at someone."

Derek's head fell into his palms, close to knee level.

"Who'd you yell at?"

"About half the store. I slipped on some lettuce and yelled at the cooks. I about ran into a server and yelled at her. Then... Kat, I screwed up big."

She took his hand. "You still have your job, right?"

He huffed. "Actually, they offered me a promotion."

"A promotion? Then you couldn't have screwed up too much." She leaned back into the couch.

"I did. I got after Michelle while she was handling a situation where the police should have been called. Some guy swatted a server on the butt, and other than the guy having to leave, nothing happened because of me."

The silence stretched between them for several seconds. Why didn't she say something? It only made things harder.

"Is the server okay?"

"She's really shaken up. I apologized to everyone but..."

She placed her hand on his back. "What else can you do?"

He shrugged in response.

"You can't do anything more, just don't let it happen again. That's it."

"You make everything sound so easy."

"Yeah, I'm pretty cool that way. So, a promotion?"

Darkness surrounded Kat as she tried to stifle her thoughts in bed. With Derek's arm stretched around her, and he snored softly in her ear. No matter how hard she tried to stop thinking, moisture built up in her eyes over his outburst. Not to mention moving.

He'd seriously lost his temper in a way she'd never witnessed. At work. Because of Joey. The idea of him losing control because of their son pounded inside of her, refusing to quiet. The baseball game from months ago flooded her mind. His anger got the best of him there too.

Embarrassment often caused him to overreact. What kind of relationship could he have with Joey if Joey constantly embarrassed him? What kind of marriage could they have?

She pushed at the ruminations, urging them to leave, to allow her to rest and move on until her emotions were less fragile, but their strength overpowered hers.

When does trust turn to distrust? When does love twist into hate? Kat shifted out from under Derek's arm and sought her way through the dark room to the kitchen. Moving a few cans of beans and franks, she reached for her hidden chocolate stash. No one ever moved the beans and franks.

The smooth candy never rid her mind of such things, but it made them easier to think. That's what she told herself, anyway.

She'd never reflected on what might cause her to leave Derek. When her mother brought it up, it had nothing to do with Kat's frustrations. Instead, she suggested patience and offered the notion that Kat should protect Derek from an autistic three-year-old.

Abuse. She'd leave over abuse, right?

She couldn't imagine Derek hitting either of them. He'd never so much as spanked Joey. Not until after the diagnosis, just before the baseball game. She'd forgotten about that. Almost. He'd spanked Joey's leg. The anger she saw in Derek's eyes that day flashed through her mind. Would he have stopped if she hadn't called to him? Would he do it again?

She had spanked Joey once. Discouragement ran through her veins that day. She'd sworn to never spank again, even if it was legal, and she hadn't.

Closing her eyes, she shook her head. Tucson. She flung her head back against the couch as fresh tears bubbled in her eyes. She squeezed them tighter, then blinked until they stayed open.

Joey finally had the help he needed. Picking up and starting in a different county with different therapists and a different school? In theory, transferring meant starting up again in a week, maybe less. The services provided came from the state, not the county, but some of the services were county-run. She'd have to check with Ms. Coach about transferring schools. Would his IEP be accepted?

She did not want to move, but how could she tell her husband to turn down a promotion with a forty-percent raise? Who does that? Less than three hours away, but it changed everything.

She finished her chocolate.

"Kat, what're you doing?" Derek flicked on the hall light as he shuffled toward the living room.

"Sneaking chocolate."

"Gonna share?"

"It's gone."

He sat next to her. "You only move those cans when something's bothering you."

She eyed him. "You know about my stash?"

"Yes." A corner of his mouth eased up.

"Great. Now I have to find a new hiding place."

A tear rolled past her chin, dropping to her hands as her facade cracked.

"So…"

"I can't move, Derek. The idea of getting Joey setup somewhere else, having to find new people, moving farther from my parents."

"When was the last time you visited your parents?"

"Forever ago." A chuckle stuck in her throat. "That's not the point. I have no desire to move, but how can I ask you to turn down a forty-percent raise or even the opportunity?"

"You're my wife. We make these decisions together."

"I'm mean. I want the money, but I don't want to move. What will Steve say to that?"

"I don't know. But it would mean a lot of commuting. Most of the stores are down there."

She slapped her knees. "Of course they are!" she said, as she shot to her feet and sliced the thick fog around her with the wave of her arm.

"If you don't want to move—"

"I can't ask that of you."

"As much as I haven't shown it recently, I still want to look after my family."

"Well, your family needs to support you too."

"Come to bed, Kat. This is not a conversation for three in the morning."

"I need more chocolate."

Derek held his hand out to her. "You're out, unless you lied to me."

"Dang." She clung to his hand without knowing what would happen, but his willingness to listen to her helped lighten her concern about moving. The other problems she'd have to figure out on her own.

Derek waited for Kat to sit down for dinner. He'd spent several days considering the Baja Holiday Picnic. A family affair, the picnic took place in a pavilion at one of the valley's large parks. Several kiddie rides dotted a small amusement area, including a train ride. The outdoors helped disperse crowds and noise, but taking Joey meant a probable meltdown and the possibility of missing the awards ceremony. That couldn't happen. Joey loved trains and small rides, but never lasted at a park for more than an hour. It took forty minutes to drive there. For some reason, corporate deemed the East Valley park better fitting for their needs.

Intruder number three had made quite the impression on Kat, and he hoped she would consider asking Mindi—Mandie—to watch Joey during the picnic. If Kat struggled to leave Joey home with Mandie, Derek planned to invite her along, pending Kat's approval. Getting an award sounded so nice in theory.

Kat puttered around the kitchen, making Derek worry that Mandie might finish Joey's bath before they'd had a chance to talk.

"Come sit down."

"I will. Give me a minute to get some of this stuff taken care of first. It makes it easier to do the dishes later."

"Your food's getting cold."

She rolled her eyes. "So's yours. Go ahead and eat."

He lifted his fork of instant mashed potatoes to his mouth, letting it hover there before dropping it back to his plate.

"Mandie's done a great job with Joey, hasn't she?"

Kat straightened her back and put the box of potato flakes back on the counter.

"I love her. She's attentive, responsible. I've learned more than I ever imagined, and she's not here for me." Her smile brightened, and she picked up her plate of food, moving to the table. "I don't know what I'd do without her."

"Good. That's what Joey needs. You too." He forced the bite of potatoes into his mouth. "So, have you tried leaving him with her? I know you've liked the idea of grocery shopping without him."

She shook her head and swallowed. "No. I get my shopping done when he's at school."

"What about going out with friends?"

"What friends? I haven't had friends since he was born."

"Oh, come on, I've seen you talk with other women at the park."

"You mean strangers?" She laughed. "I never even learn their names. I have no friends. Well, except you."

Another bite of food, this time he tried the meat-looking stuff. "What happened to Melanie and Steph?"

"Nothing. They got busy with their lives like I got busy with mine."

"Maybe one day you ladies can get together again."

The hard road, now he knew.

"Listen, this picnic coming up, I'm getting an award."

"Yeah."

"It's a big deal. I'm the only one receiving anything, and the CEO..."

She eyed him, and he lost his train of thought. Why couldn't she make this easy?

He cleared his throat. "Joey struggles with crowds and noise, and I thought it might be better if he—"

"No."

"No? I didn't finish."

"I'm not leaving him with Mandie. No."

"You just told me how much you love her, how attentive she is."

Kat stood up. "She is, but I'm not ready to leave him. His finger's barely healed."

"It's been, at minimum, six weeks." He shook his head. Arguing accomplished nothing. "No matter. We don't have to leave him. Let's bring Mandie along. We can do that, right?"

She rushed around the kitchen, haphazardly scraping dishes and swiping at the counter with a rag. "I don't want to."

"Why?" His voice softened considerably as he stood from the table and wound his arms around her, stopping her cleaning rampage.

"All those other women. They'd think I can't handle my own child."

Her body shuddered in his arms.

"No one thinks that at all. Why would—"

"Because Mandie comes across as a nanny. I'm a stay-at-home mom, Derek. Not a rich one, a middle-class, cleans her own house, takes care of her kid kind of stay-at-home mom. If Mandie goes, I...I look like a failure."

Derek lifted her chin. "I don't know how to respond. You're saying you're embarrassed? Like me?"

Kat jerked away. "Not like you. I'm not embarrassed by my son. I'm embarrassed by what others might think of me."

"Yeah, like me."

She threw the rag onto the counter. "It's not the same, Derek. You're embarrassed by Joey's actions. I'm embarrassed by my own."

"So, you want to get rid of the intruders?" He tried to lighten his tone.

"No. But I don't want to have them do my job when I'm available to do it myself."

"And when you need a break? You need those too, you know."

She frowned. "He goes to school two days a week. I get twenty hours a month."

"Does my opinion come into play in this matter at all?" He stared at her. "My company's picnic, where I'm receiving an award?"

Her bottom lip trembled as she walked past him. "I can't, Derek. I just can't. I'm sorry."

Picnic Panic

Several days passed, as had several arguments. And what good did it do? Neither Kat nor Derek was happy.

Now, the night before the Baja Holiday Picnic, Kat shut the bedroom door and locked it before flinging herself onto her bed. Tears streamed into her pillow as she muffled her gasping cries. She'd always figured people only cried like that when a loved one died or some other debilitating monstrosity occurred. Not so. Autism caused it too—in a way. That, or marriage.

The sobs strengthened. Autism now lined her life forever. What did that mean for her marriage? Two realizations flooded her mind simultaneously. She wouldn't back down when it came to leaving Joey home from the picnic or taking Mandie. And thinking about the health of her marriage served no purpose, not when autism still overwhelmed her.

Disheartening notions continued to consume her as she considered the last week.

After several days of telling Derek no, Kat had suggested she stay home with Joey. After all, Derek obviously didn't want their son with them, and she refused to put Joey in danger by leaving him with someone else.

Then there was the thought of taking Mandie to the picnic and facing the few women who shared her chosen lifestyle. It made her stomach churn. The choice to stay home and raise her son involved sacrificing a two-income household and taking care of her son, not taking paid help along when it got hard. It didn't matter that she didn't personally pay anyone. Some would call it worse. Mandie's paycheck came from the government—from tax-payer funds. Accepting therapy was one thing, but public babysitting? No.

She groaned, clutching the pillow tighter.

The second she'd suggested staying home with Joey, Derek's tightened muscles made his opinion clear. With her knee bouncing wildly, she'd accepted that she and Joey would attend the picnic. What other choice did she have? As long as she refused to budge in favor of Derek's desires, all other doors were bolted shut.

Saturday morning came too early, but Kat climbed out of bed and readied herself and Joey while Derek sprawled on the bed reading a book.

"What time do we need to leave?" she asked.

"It starts at ten." His flat tone echoed the lingering tension that had clouded their home for so long.

"I'm sorry I'm failing you as a wife."

Derek glared at her. "That's not passive aggressive at all."

"Good, it wasn't meant to be. Just flippant." She stood there for a minute, fighting her inner demons. "You're getting an award today. I think it might be time to get along."

"We're getting along fine."

"Sure. That's why I can't walk through the house without losing my way in a cloud of hostility."

"I think I have some old fog lights in the garage." The corner of his mouth lifted slightly.

"Those might help." She sat on the bed next to him. "I can't keep fighting like this."

The rigidity in his jaw loosened. "This week's been hard."

"Not only this week, Derek. It's been months."

His hand rested on her back. Tingles still ran up her spine when he did that.

"Let's have a good time today, huh?" she said. "We can ride the train, maybe visit Santa Claus."

"He's terrified of Santa," Derek said.

She shifted, pushing her fist against her leg. "That's true. No Santa."

He nodded.

"I bought Joey a little fishing pole and picked up some duck pellets too."

"Duck pellets?" His brow lifted.

"They're better for the ducks."

Kat leaned closer to him, enjoying the smile lines that only appeared when he was sincere. A week without his smile had been a long time. Too long.

"I think we can manage feeding the ducks, but what about when Joey falls apart?" Derek asked.

"Then, I take him to a quiet place and help calm him down. We both do if you're free."

She kissed him before standing up, but settled back down on the bed when he caught her hand. "Is there any way we can keep him happy when I receive my award? I don't want you to miss it."

His arms wrapped around her waist, coaxing her closer. She missed feeling close to him.

"I hope so." She leaned toward him. "I can't wait to see you walk up there as the only guy capable of training an entire store in six weeks."

Gently pressing on her back, Derek lowered her lips to his. Kat breathed in the warm kiss, reveling in her husband's love.

"Maybe not the only guy," he said.

"Definitely the only guy."

This time when she stood, he let her go.

"You better hurry, it's nine-thirty," she said.

After an hour-long drive, Kat stepped out of the car into the December breeze. The first crisp deciduous leaves fluttered to the ground, landing on the last remnants of green grass, while evergreens of all kinds provided thin wisps of shade. The highs hovered in the upper-seventies. She couldn't have asked for a better day to bring Joey to the park.

As she helped her son out of his seat, she peeked at Derek. He rocked on the balls of his feet and fidgeted with the sides of his pants, his thumbs hooked into his side pockets. He was nervous. She and Joey rounded the car, and Derek picked up their son.

"Let's check in real fast, then we should be able to relax a bit," he said.

She nodded as she slung her bag with the heavy duck pellets onto her shoulder. Together they walked to the large ramada where a group of people congregated around shaded metal tables. The towering desert pines and mesquite trees provided sparse shade nearby. Some of the kids from the group climbed the trees, while others played a game of tag.

As Joey scanned the area with wide eyes, Kat realized how much he wanted to play too. Strolling toward the other kids, she let go of his hand and allowed him to play at his own level. He ran around in circles.

One of the other children touched him, yelling, "You're it!"

Joey stopped and stared at the boy. Worry tightened Kat's brow. She wanted Joey to participate, but he had no idea how. After taking a step forward, she paused.

A girl, who appeared to be six or seven, stood next to Joey. "It's easy. Chase us, and when you touch somebody, yell *you're it*."

Joey stared at her, and clasping his hand, she tried another approach.

"Come on, I'll help you!"

Joey ran beside her, and as they approached another child, she looked at Joey and said, "Touch him."

Joey reached out his hand and touched the boy's arm, who had allowed himself to be caught.

"Now say, *you're it*," the girl instructed.

Joey mumbled "you're it" and the older girl directed him away from the boy he'd tagged.

The giggle floating from Joey's little body brightened Kat's smile. How did the little girl know what her son needed?

"Kat." Derek waved her over from a few feet away.

Checking on Joey one more time, she stepped toward to Derek and the balding man next to him.

"You remember Steve, the guy who keeps me on my toes and tells me to train one store as I manage another."

"I do. It's nice to see you again," she said, working to keep her focus on Steve and Derek during the time her husband needed her to. "This is a beautiful park."

"I think so too. My wife and I used to bring our children here when they were younger—for the train rides. Where's your little guy?"

"He's playing tag with the other kids."

She positioned herself where she could watch Joey better as she pointed him out to Steve.

"Cute little guy. Derek tells me he has some delays?"

"Autism."

When neither Steve nor Derek said anything, she shifted uncomfortably and spoke again.

"He receives several therapies and preschool. He's doing really well."

"Fantastic," Steve said before turning back to Derek and changing the subject.

As she turned to walk back to Joey, Kat felt a hand on her shoulder and stopped.

"Kat, it's so good to see you."

"Hi, Lisa, how have you been?" Kat's muscles tightened with the desire to return to Joey.

The wife of a corporate guru and a stay-at-home mom like herself, Lisa always tracked Kat down at Baja events.

"Oh, I've been great. Mitch and I moved to the West Side a few months ago, and Bailey started kindergarten. She's so advanced, we think she might be able to skip a grade. You know, she's not supposed to start until next year, but we got her into a program for students with late birthdays. If she does well enough, they'll move her right up to first grade."

"That's fantastic."

"Well, we worked hard with her at home. She can already count to twenty-five."

Kat nodded as she watched Joey.

"I'm sure you're working with your little boy too. Does he have a late birthday?"

"No. He was born in March."

"How old is he? Did you bring him today?"

Kat pointed toward Joey. "He's three."

As Lisa spotted Joey, she swallow deeply and a wobble entered her voice. "Isn't he something. Is he having a hard time potty training?"

"Yeah. We're working on it."

"Bailey potty-trained early, I think. She was two and a half. Girls usually finish earlier than boys."

Kat realized the woman was trying to sympathize, but potty training hardly hit her list of daily concerns. "He'll get there. I'm not worried."

"Of course you're not."

"I promised Joey we'd feed the ducks. I better get him before his patience runs out."

"I understand completely. Don't miss Santa. He'll be here anytime."

"Okay." Kat was learning to perfect her placating smile.

"Great. We can chat more later." Lisa waved.

Hurrying over to Joey, Kat hoped to avoid any other moms with advanced children.

Though she could have told Lisa that Joey counts to one hundred in his sleep, she withheld the information. She saw no reason to participate in ridiculous I.Q. competitions. Besides, once Joey's autism breached conversations, his I.Q. swirled into nothingness. He'd be the boy with a disability, not the advanced boy who could count to one hundred.

When Kat approached the children, Joey ran up and gave her a hug. She knelt beside him. "Do you want to go feed the ducks?"

He gazed at the water with a calm demeanor.

Kat dug in her bag to pull out the duck pellets as the girl from earlier walked over and stood next to Joey.

"What's his name?"

"Joey." Kat smiled at the girl. "Thank you for helping him play."

"I like helping people."

"That's good."

The girl peered at Joey, then back at Kat, something clearly on her mind. "He doesn't talk very much, does he?"

"Not much."

"How come?"

"Talking is hard for him. But he's learning to talk more."

"Oh. I have a hard time tying my shoes. Can he do that?"

"Not yet, but I'm sure he'll learn, just like you will. We all have a hard time learning sometimes, don't we?"

"Yup." The girl ran back to the other children, fully accepting of Joey.

With the duck pellets in hand, Kat used big arm movements to gain Derek's attention, then she and Joey walked to the ducks.

No starved ducks swam in the park's cement-edged pond. A few pellets hit the water, and ducks of all colors and sizes rushed toward them. Joey giggled each time he tossed pellets into the water. He especially liked it when the ducks popped up after swimming under the surface.

Because of his other responsibilities, it took Derek five minutes to appear. Schmoozing the bosses left less time with family. Yet Derek shook the hands of people who had no more interest in talking with him than he had in talking to them. Kat understood how it worked.

Derek picked up Joey and swung him onto his shoulders, then handed him some pellets. "Throw them far."

When the pellets fell at his feet and a land-bound duck rushed over for the feast, Joey gasped, then settled into a soft giggle.

"Looks like everything's going well. He's having fun?" Derek asked.

"He is." Kat scattered a few pellets into the water, enjoying their feathered friends as much as her son. "Did you see him playing tag?"

"I did."

"That little girl who helped him was so cute. I'm glad she was there."

"I saw you talking to Lisa. That's her name, right?"

"Yes. She's Mitch's wife."

"How'd it go?"

Kat rolled her eyes. "About how I expected. Her daughter is enrolled in a program that will allow her to skip her real year of kindergarten and advance into first grade early."

"What grade is she in now?"

"Kindergarten. She repeats it if she isn't advanced enough to move forward. Lisa is convinced she'll advance though. She counts to twenty-five."

Derek laughed. "Women are weird."

"Not all of us," Kat muttered. "She tumbled over her words once she realized Joey isn't potty-trained."

"Ignore her."

"I know."

Joey wiggled to get down, and Derek set him on the ground.

"Wanna go climb a tree, buddy?"

Dad and son raced toward a tree in the center of an open area. Joey, clutching the bark with both hands, tried to step into the low V of the trunk. Derek hoisted him up and helped him stand in the V, then slowly lifted his body to one of the lower branches. Mesquite leaves caught in Joey's hair as his head brushed past them. Kat dug out her phone and took a couple of pictures, happy at how wonderful the day had turned out.

Once Joey was out of the tree, the three of them spent some time at the playground. But, while on the swings, Joey's head popped up at the sound of the train whistle. He watched intently as the train, crowded with people of all ages, left the station and traveled around the park. Squirming, he struggled to get out of the baby swing.

Luckily, Kat had already purchased tickets and soon held them up for him to see, one for each of them to ride the next train. Derek grinned and helped Joey down from the swing. Little legs carried the boy to Kat, who waited at the edge of the playground. She knelt down next to him.

"Joey, we have to stand in line, okay? It's going to take some time."

Joey refused to meet her eyes, staring intently at the train station. Holding hands, with Joey in the middle, they all walked together.

The pocket-sized amusement area bustled with big and little bodies, all of them waiting for their turn to ride the train. Small giggles and boisterous laughter abounded, none of it appearing to bother Joey.

After ten minutes, the train returned. Kat clutched Joey's hand and steered him toward the entrance, only to find the rope hung immediately in front of them.

"Sorry, we're full. The next train leaves in fifteen minutes."

The skinny teenage boy strolled back toward the snack bar and ticket booth.

Little furrowed brows formed on Joey's face, and he scowled at the rope.

"We'll go in a bit, okay, buddy," Derek said, as he knelt next to Joey. "That's not very long, and we can wave at the train as it passes."

"Joey want train."

Kat brushed at the mesquite leaves still sprinkled through her son's hair. "You can ride the train next. We can sit anywhere you want because you'll be the first one on. Where do you want to sit?"

She pointed at the various cars on the train. Most appeared about the same, bright orange or blue, some green or yellow. At the back of the train followed a red caboose, complete with barred windows.

Talking to Joey about the train helped some, but his mood soon deteriorated. Derek leaned down and lifted him up. Following the example of Kat and Mandie, he rubbed a firm hand from Joey's neck down his back. A paralyzing scream echoed throughout the train station, as Joey kicked his feet and shoved Derek. Kat jumped, hurrying to take their son in her arms as he catapulted himself backward.

"He sounds hurt."

"He's not hurt." Derek scoffed. "I rubbed his back."

"I know, but he only cries like then when he's hurt."

"Kat, he's angry. Take him for a walk, and I'll stay in line and wait for the train."

She exited the line, Joey screeching louder by the minute. Nothing consoled him, and he refused to talk. When the train came back, he quieted; though, he still clung to Kat. When Derek climbed into a car, he began howling again.

"I think he wants the caboose." Kat walked toward the back, Derek dragging his feet behind.

Joey curled into Kat as the train left the station, but when Derek leaned over and patted his back, he started screaming again.

"Something's wrong, Derek. He doesn't cry like this when he gets what he wants."

"He's overwhelmed and angry he had to wait for the train. That's all."

Kat searched Joey's neck and back, checking his arms and legs. The train's movement and shaded caboose made it difficult to see anything.

"Did something bite him? Were there ants in that tree?"

"Nothing bit him."

With Joey screaming, the conversation ended, and Kat silently ran through every scenario. Nothing. Yet, his little face reddened as large drops fell from his eyes. Derek helped Kat and Joey off the train, even as tension overtook his jaw and his eyes darkened. "They're serving lunch. Will he eat anything?"

"Are you hungry, Joey? Should we get some food?"

The crying didn't stop, and Kat shook her head unknowingly.

"Let's try eating," Derek said.

People gaped as they left the amusement area and hurried further into the park instead of toward a car. Kat rarely noticed gawkers, but this time it appeared everyone in the park wanted to know what they had done to Joey.

She bit her lip as she weighed the options in front of them. "Derek," she said, "why don't you get some food, and we'll sit at the back table away from everyone else so the noise doesn't interfere too much."

"What do I get him?"

"Chips, soda, chicken... What are they serving?"

"I'm not sure."

"Do your best to find something. He loves chips. I'd start there."

She sat on the bench of the table and held Joey, who still clung to her. Usually, anything other than deep pressure bothered him during a meltdown. Now he wanted anything but deep pressure.

"Joey, are you hurt? What happened? Why are you sad?"

Each question she asked went unanswered. Glancing up to check Derek's position at the serving tables, she swallowed deeply.

Lisa rushed to her, Bailey following. "My, he's not having a good time, is he? Is it because he missed Santa, or does he need a diaper change?"

"He can get overwhelmed with crowds."

Kat refused to meet Lisa's eyes, wishing she would leave.

Unfortunately, the woman bent down and placed her hand on Joey's back, who screamed louder in response.

"Hey little guy, it's time to stop crying and let your mommy have a break."

Kat let Lisa continue for a bit, but the more she spoke to Joey, the more aggravated he became.

"It's best to leave him alone when he gets like this."

Lisa raised an eyebrow. "Does this happen a lot?"

"It can."

"I don't think that's normal, Kat. Let me get you the name of Bailey's pediatrician."

Kat stood up and searched for Derek, but couldn't find him anywhere. Joey kept shrieking in her ear, and talking to Lisa drove her quicker toward the edge.

"I think it's best if we go find a place away from people. Tell Derek for me, okay?"

At the last minute, she snapped up her bag and dashed away from the ramada.

A quick walk later and settled on a bench away from others, Kat pulled out the phone and texted Derek their location.

Derek: *COME BACK. The award ceremony is starting*

Kat: *He's still screaming*

Derek: *I knew this would happen*

Joey whipped his head back with a wail. Kat texted back: *Something's WRONG*

Derek: *We should have left him home*

Kat tossed her phone back into her bag, and focused her attention on Joey. His cries softened, but the tears continued. A moment more, and his breathing sounded off, wheezy.

Kat lunged off the bench, leaving everything but Joey behind, and ran toward the ramada. Derek stood on the makeshift stage, and Kat bolted to the front where she yelled, "He's not breathing right. We need to go now!"

Derek's eyes pierced hers, infuriated. "Kat."

"I'm sorry. But something's wrong!"

She laid Joey on the ground, noticing the copious amount of moisture. Sweat, not tears. She fumbled with his shirt when one of the many people who came to her aid called out, "Scorpion!"

She followed the pointing finger to see a small, dead scorpion coiled in the crook of her son's collar.

"No! Derek!" She clutched Joey, lifting him to her. "Call an ambulance—he can't breathe! I told you something was wrong, that he was hurt!"

A second later, Lisa touched Kat's back.

"They're on their way."

Kat nodded, hoping her eyes conveyed the gratitude she felt for this woman who annoyed her so deeply.

Derek leaped down to Kat and Joey, his face pale. "I didn't know."

"You didn't care, Derek!"

When the EMTs arrived, they immediately administered oxygen and loaded Joey onto a gurney. "Ma'am, you can ride in the back with me to help keep him calm. Can you do that? Otherwise, I'll have you sit up front."

Kat climbed into the back of the ambulance, promising to stay out of the way while avoiding Derek's heartbroken demeanor. As one of the EMTs passed him, Derek reached out to catch his attention.

"He's my son. What hospital are you going to?"

"Closest is Carson's."

Kat watched Derek drop his gaze as the ambulance doors closed. He deserved to suffer. How could he have ignored her? She'd spent more time with their son than he ever had. She knew something was wrong. How could he ignore that—disregard everything she'd said? Had he not been there, Joey would have already reached the hospital.

Derek sprang into his car. Steve had tried to speak to him before he rushed to the hospital, but he'd brushed his boss' hand away, shoving past him.

"Steve, I have to go now."

The car's engine shuddered with Derek's frantic urging to accelerate faster. All those times Joey melted down over nothing—why hadn't he listened to Kat? A stupid award. No good parent put an award above their child. Kat would never forgive him. He wasn't certain he could forgive himself. She was right; he hadn't cared. He'd wanted to come first for a change. That worked out well. Now an ambulance sped toward the hospital with his dying son and his unforgiving wife. He didn't blame her for hating him. He only hoped she'd let him try to make amends.

Tears blurred his vision. Wiping them away, he clenched his fists tighter on the steering wheel. His marriage was over—she'd leave—he had no doubt.

In the parking lot, Derek sucked air into his lungs through lamenting cries before exiting the car.

Scorpion.

Why hadn't he thought of that? The colder air decreased their numbers, but they still crawled out occasionally, especially on trees. Bark scorpions—some of the most venomous—life threatening to young children. How? Why hadn't he listened?

Oh Kat, forgive me, please forgive me.

The hospital doors slid open as Derek ran into the ER and scanned the room, eyes wide, until he spotted the reception desk. In his agony he'd forgotten that emergency rooms came with waiting rooms, unlike some on TV. "My son—"

"Name?"

"Der—Joey Burns. He was stung by a scorpion."

"Yes, sir. May I see some I.D.?" The receptionist typed on her computer with long, purple fingernails.

"If you'll step to the door on your right, someone will escort you back."

"Thank you." Derek moved toward another sliding glass door.

A young man wearing blue scrubs met Derek and walked him through empty halls to another secure door. Derek's heart raced, anxiousness to see Joey and apologize to Kat coursing through his body. What kind of apology could he give? Certainly not a good enough one. He blinked back tears as he entered another hallway before being taken to a curtained area.

A bag hung from the pole next to Joey's bed, IV fluids flowing into his arm that rested motionless next to his sleeping body. Derek rushed to the side of the bed and kissed his son's forehead as tears cascaded unabashedly to the white sheets.

"I'm so sorry," he whispered. "Joey, I'm so, so sorry. I should have known. I never should have put you in that tree. Kat"—he lifted his eyes to meet his wife's glower—"Kat, I should have listened to you. This...everything, it's all my fault. I can't believe I didn't listen, I—"

"I can."

Acrimony still laced her voice, creating deep lines around her mouth.

"You cared about Joey until the doctor said he had autism, then your devotion disappeared. A switch flipped, and you stopped. How does a parent stop loving their child, Derek? How? I understand that autism is hard; I really do, but...but you just refused to see it, refused to admit it existed. And then you refused to see that your little boy was hurt, not angry, not tantruming. Hurt!"

She paused, but Derek remained quiet. As the vein in her temple stopped beating in time with her breathing, he prepared to listen. Anything she said he deserved.

"A scorpion!" she yelled. "He could have died! We barely made it here in time. His face and neck swelled, and they had to administer epinephrine. Adrenaline, Derek. You're right. This is your fault."

She lowered her face into her palms and shook her head.

"Leave."

The word softly escaped her lips, and Derek wasn't sure he'd heard her. She rose to her feet, rolling her shoulders back.

"Leave. I can't stand the sight of you. Leave Derek."

"Kat, I..."

Her fingers brushed the sides of her pants as she swiftly raised her arm and pointed at the exit.

"Leave, now! I don't want you here. I don't want y... Just leave, now!"

Another young man in scrubs walked past, and embarrassment roiled through Derek's blood. His head hung to his chest, as he tried to find the words to save his marriage.

"I'm sorry."

Kat sat down, turning away from him.

"I don't care." The words were soft, but their meaning echoed through the halls.

Tears filled his eyes again, and he leaned down toward Joey to give him a kiss goodbye.

"Don't you touch him."

The growling words struck him with force, but he ignored them. Even if it meant putting himself first one last time, he couldn't leave his son without saying goodbye.

Brushing the hair from Joey's forehead, he trailed his finger down the side of his little face and cheek, the softness of his skin oddly comforting. Then he lowered his lips to his son's warm forehead, holding the position as he breathed in the sweetness.

"I love you," he said. "I love both of you."

Without facing Kat, Derek staggered beyond the curtain and out of the room.

Kat's Denial

Those who sleep on their backs may find some comfort in vinyl recliners, but Kat found it excruciating. So when the doctor entered the temporary room, sitting up came easily to her.

"Joey's mom?"

"Yes."

The doctor studied a clipboard in his hand before looking up at Kat. He held out his hand. "Unlucky thing, getting stung by a scorpion in December. Unusual too. Most of them are hibernating."

Kat stared at him flatly.

"Would have been worse if he'd run into a nest. Crazy little critters, all grouped together to stay warm."

She raised an eyebrow.

He dropped the clipboard to his side. "I'd like to keep Joey here overnight. The short shelf life of epinephrine can cause symptoms to return in a few patients, and I'd rather not risk sending Joey home."

"Thank you." Kat sighed in relief.

"Great. So, do you have any questions for me?"

"Is his life still in danger?"

A corner of the doctor's mouth rose, dropping fast. "No. We're equipped to take care of anything else that might happen. Like I said, at most it would be symptoms returning. That requires another shot, nothing more."

Kat nodded.

"Anything else?"

"I wouldn't mind an extra blanket."

"We're going to go ahead and move you to a room for the night, shouldn't take more than a minute. I'll let the nurse know you'd like a blanket."

Less than a quarter hour passed before Kat peeked into the semi-private room to see another little boy lying quietly in bed watching TV while his defeated-looking mother slept in a chair. A curtain separating the beds waited open for someone to pull it across for privacy. The notion of those few steps exhausted Kat, and she settled into the plastic recliner next to Joey's bed and curled into the provided blanket without another thought.

Soon after, a knock sounded at the door, and Lisa followed a bouquet of flowers into the room. Kat tried to smile, but failed. Instead, she watched as Lisa pulled the curtain between the children's beds closed, then sat in a folding chair next to Kat.

"How is he?"

Tears formed in Kat's eyes, the comfort Lisa brought into the room catching her off guard. "He's okay. The doctor's keeping him for observation, that's all."

"Where's your husband?"

Kat pursed her lips as she worked to keep her knee still. "I told him to leave. I can't..."

Lisa rubbed her back. "It feels like he hurt your son, I understand. You'll work it out."

"Yeah, but I can stay mad for now, right?" A lone chuckle escaped Kat's lips.

"Absolutely."

"I can't believe I interrupted the award ceremony. The whole thing meant the world to Derek."

"Something tells me that's the last thing on his mind right now."

"You didn't see the rage on his face when I called to him."

"I think we all saw it, but we also saw the distress when he realized what had happened."

"He brushed me off, telling me Joey was angry he didn't get what he wanted." Kat gazed into Lisa's eyes. "A scorpion. I checked his shirt four times before whoever-it-was spotted it."

Lisa patted her back, letting her speak.

"All Derek had to do was listen to me. That's it—maybe take the time to help me check. Do you know how hard it is to look for a bite or a sting or anything when your child doesn't want his back or neck touched?"

"I can imagine. Does he usually let you touch him?" Lisa waved her hands in front of her, showing

209

Kat she wanted to explain the question. "I heard he has autism and know some kids with autism don't, right?"

Someone told her after Kat had purposefully remained silent. Figures.

"Yeah, some don't. Joey does okay with most of it though."

Lisa smiled. "I'm glad. I don't think I could handle it if Bailey didn't let me hug her."

"Me either."

"When did you find out—about the autism, I mean."

"April." Kat dropped her face into her hands as sobs racked through her body, then she sat up and continued. "It's tearing my family apart. All of it. I hate it! My husband doesn't understand my son. I don't understand my son! We have therapists and coordinators and meetings that make no sense. I try to learn, but everyone says the same thing: *it depends on the child.* What does that even mean?"

"I think it means you're a parent."

Kat studied Lisa for several seconds. "It's more than that." The flat words rumbled in her chest.

"Maybe. I know there's a lot going on in your life. You're learning something new about your son, and I get the impression your son isn't the type who sits on the couch watching cartoons all day or picks up his toys when you ask."

"No. He's the one unscrewing doors from their hinges or screaming because he doesn't like the way you poured his juice."

Lisa nodded. "Well, I know nothing about that, but I do know about helping my child after she's had a nighttime accident or the desperation she feels when she isn't perfect. I know what it's like to want to hold her in my arms and protect her from the world only to realize I can't."

She took Kat's hand. "I'm still figuring this parenting thing out too. Bailey's only five, but from what I've seen, no two children are alike, not even identical twins. We all struggle."

The corner of Kat's mouth lifted. "I've never thought of it that way."

Hours ago, she hated this woman and her excelling child. To her, they boasted and flapped their pretty little wings for attention. Being wrong smarted. Yet no one knew Kat's erring notions, but everyone knew Derek's blunder.

Kat blinked. "That makes a lot of sense—thinking of it as children instead of children with autism."

"Glad I could help." Lisa stood and rummaged through her purse. "I brought this little train for Joey. I hope he likes it."

Now, Kat rose to her feet and tugged Lisa into a hug. "I don't know how to thank you for everything."

"There's nothing to thank me for. These are the things we do for friends."

Another quick hug, and Lisa walked out of the room, and Kat tried, once again, to find comfort in the vinyl chair next to her sleeping son. Flicking her feet up, she lowered her head. It didn't take long before she readjusted the back and lowered the feet slightly.

Her mind flitted through everything she'd said to Derek. Nothing kind. Eight months seemed hardly enough time to figure parenting out, let alone autism.

Holding her charging phone, she counted rings, waiting for Derek to pick up. No answer. She peered at the clock and tried again. Derek often went to bed before ten, but she really needed to talk to him. Why wouldn't he answer? Giving up, she texted: *I'm sorry. I overreacted. Love U.*

With the phone back on the metal table, Kat rested her head on the padded vinyl chair. This time, even as the chair stuck to her legs and her head either felt too high or too low, she fell into a restless sleep.

The next morning, Kat waited impatiently for the doctor to release Joey. Derek's only text told her where to find the car, and he refused to answer any of her calls. With the paperwork finally finished, she considered heading to the restaurant before home, but remembered Derek had the day off.

Joey played with the train Lisa had dropped off as she buckled him into his car seat. How like Derek to leave the car for her despite her unkindness. Brushing Joey's hair off his forehead, she wondered at her son's dance with death. Had he not received the epinephrine when he did, he would have… She didn't want to think about it. Not really.

"Joey, should we go see Daddy?"

He looked up from the toy, a faint smile crossing his lips.

Kat slipped into the driver's seat and gripped the steering wheel, praying an appropriate apology might float through her mind on the way home. Derek still had a lot to learn, but questioning his love for Joey wasn't fair. Kat knew the truth. He loved them. Both of them, regardless of mistakes, behaviors, or disabilities.

Her heart pounded in her chest as she contemplated how close she had come to telling Derek that she didn't want him. She'd stopped herself. After all, the idea of living without Derek broke her heart in two. Only the pain of living without him, happiness depleted, could flit through her imagination.

Once home, Kat slumped in her seat. Derek's side of the driveway was empty. Arms falling to her lap, she sat for a moment before unbuckling Joey and taking him inside. Seeing and talking to Derek had whirled through her mind so much, she wasn't sure what to do after finding him gone.

Joey walked to the couch and pushed his train along the cushions, and Kat ruffled his hair as she picked up the phone one more time, calling Derek. He didn't answer, again. She paced the house, opening the fridge and a couple of cabinets. She flipped the TV off almost as quickly as she turned it on. Concerned the flooring in the main part of the house might wear out under her feet, she changed direction and trod into her bedroom.

A single piece of paper on the bed drew her attention. She must have forgotten to throw away a scrap. Thinking nothing of it, she grabbed it off the bed, preparing to throw it away after a cursory glance, but she paused instead.

Sinking to the bed, she read the short note.

Kat,

I can't keep putting you through this. You or Joey. I've taken everything I need with me and will have papers served to you, so don't concern yourself with it. Don't worry, you can have full custody and the house. I'll send as much money as I can every month. The savings is yours; I think there's several thousand there.

Please, Kat, I love you and Joey, but I'm no good for either of you. I have to go now. If I stayed any longer, leaving would kill me. Keep him safe and hug him often. He's my buddy.

Love You Always,
Derek

Kat dropped the note and ran to his closet, flinging the door open, she crumpled to the empty floor, sobbing.

"No, no, no, Derek, you can't leave, we need you. I need you. Please, I didn't mean it. Please." The words tumbled from her lips through tormenting cries as her hands fumbled with her phone, trying to call her husband again.

No answer.

"Answer your phone!" Echoes from the scream fought back, scratching at her eardrums.

As she focused on the floor, two small feet landed in front of her. Drawing Joey to her, she hugged him tightly, not letting go. No struggle came from his body—he seemed to understand her need.

She called Derek again and again, but no answer ever came. She left message after message, knowing he wouldn't check them. Soft clicking noises sounded as she poked at the tiny keyboard with her thumbs, hoping he'd at least read her texts. It was her only hope, and she yearned for it.

Carrying Joey, she shot out of the house and back to the car. The only place Derek ever went besides home was work. That's where he'd be.

Tires screeched out of the driveway and down the street, Kat driving chaotically until her car rested in the restaurant parking lot. Holding Joey with his legs clutching her middle, she yanked the glass door open and interrupted the hostess.

"Where's Derek?"

"I don't—isn't...isn't it his day off?"

The young girl took a step back from Kat, obviously confused.

"Yeah, but that rarely matters. I'll check the back."

Hurrying past the girl, Kat yelled *blind* as she entered the kitchen and ran to the office.

Empty.

Turning around, hot tears ran down her already warmed cheeks. Catching herself from falling, she walked out of the kitchen and stumbled toward the exit. A server took her by the elbow and questioned if she was okay.

"Where's Derek? I can't find Derek."

"Let's sit you over here, all right? I'll make some calls."

Kat fell to the bench. A few seconds later, another server brought two sodas, one in a kid's cup, and a basket of fries to the table. She nodded thanks, as she worked to control her crying.

Joey grabbed at the fries, a few landing on the floor and the bench near him. Luckily, the crowd hadn't come yet, and Joey hadn't made a peep.

"Mrs. Burns?" The server who had helped her to the table stood next to her.

So young and beautiful.

"Mrs. Burns, Derek isn't answering his phone, and I called Steve to see if he knows anything. He said Derek quit last night."

Kat's jaw dropped as she gaped at the young woman with stunned silence before violently shaking her head.

"Derek wouldn't do that. He wouldn't. He must have taken the promotion in Tucson."

"I don't think so. Steve's coming over now. He'd like to talk to you."

The young server squeezed Kat's shoulder. She knew the girl intended to console her, but Kat bumped her hand away. No twenty-year-old could understand her situation.

"Sorry. Thank you for your help. Please ask Steve to tell Derek that we can all move to Tucson."

Kat lowered Joey to the floor and staggered through the exit.

The car door closed at her side as her face strained from despair again. She'd lost count of how many times she'd cried. Lifting her phone from her purse, she dialed Derek, pleading for him to pick up.

No answer.

She crumpled over the steering wheel, reminding herself that Derek hated it when she drove upset. *I have to be safe. Joey's with me.* Breathing large gulps of air, she willed herself to calm down. A tap at her window brought her head up. Derek?

Steve.

She rolled down the window.

"Hi, Kat. How's the little guy?" Steve peered through the window at the backseat.

"He's okay now."

"Good, good. I understand you're looking for Derek."

She nodded, struggling to keep her composure. "He took the Tucson job, right?"

Steve pursed his lips before shaking his head, a sorrowful look crossing his face.

"I'm sorry. I don't know where he is. My secretary printed his resignation from an email this morning. I can't get him to answer the phone or any of my text messages." He shook his head. "I can't believe it. This isn't the Derek I know. He loves you guys."

"Yeah."

All other words refused to leave Kat's tightened throat.

"I'm sure the whole thing will blow over, and I'm not filling his position right away." Steve cleared his throat. "Even if I did, I'd find something good for him, so don't worry about that."

Kat nodded and squeaked out a thank you before rolling up the window.

Steve made sense. Derek just needed a couple of days to come to his senses.

No matter how many times the sun rose, nothing brightened Kat's days. Not with Derek gone. Five days. Five days of nothing. Five days of dilapidated marital silence.

The flattened wheel on Kat's cart thumped on the store's polished cement floor with each revolution. Why wouldn't it? Everything in her life rattled, whined, cried, and thumped out of control. A bad cart, the only one left, it fit right in.

She passed the remaining Christmas decorations. Plenty of them lined the shelves in her garage, but Derek had never taken the time to join the neighbors' festive spirits. Now she had no joy to share. Not without him.

Still, she should give Joey some sort of holiday. With tear-sodden eyes, she scanned the trees, fighting the nausea that bubbled up inside. She seized a three-foot tinseled atrocity with attached plastic bulbs and placed it in the basket. Even twenty dollars might be too much to ask, but who didn't have a tree for Christmas?

Gifts for Joey came easier. Motorcycles in every color, three different-colored and types of tape, and a large flashlight. With any luck, he wouldn't figure out how to take the flashlight apart for a week or so. The heavy-duty case and hidden battery compartment might help. But she worried that he'd find a way to the light bulb in record time.

Too bad she couldn't skip Christmas, or if nothing else, put it off until Derek got home. She ticked off the five days engraved into her mind again. Was it really taking this long to get his act together and come home? Maybe tomorrow or Saturday. What better way to make an entrance than walking in unannounced on Christmas morning?

She had the perfect picture on her phone from the company picnic. She'd print it off and frame it for Derek. They were all smiling, and Derek's grin was especially handsome as he held Joey's hand in his.

With that notion in mind, Kat throttled her thumpy cart through the store as she collected the ingredients for Derek's favorite Christmas dinner, making certain to include the sweet potatoes with pecan topping. He'd come home hungry, and this time she'd be ready.

As she arrived home, she leaned back in her seat. Joey's bus would drop him off any time, and walking inside took energy she didn't have. With her head lolled to the side, the tree in her front yard came into focus. Most of the leaves, once so green, had turned brown and fallen to the ground.

Opening her door, she wandered to the edge of the driveway where she glared at the fallen leaves. Crisp and well-formed. Whole. Fragile. One step and they'd crunch under her feet, broken into little pieces unable to be put back together.

The bus arrived, the noisy diesel engine rumbling next to her as the door slid open. The driver wished her a Merry Christmas as Joey climbed down the deep steps. She forced the corners of her mouth up, remembering her social graces, and waved goodbye.

"Did you have a good day?"

Joey nodded.

"Good! I went shopping."

She swallowed the sour taste in her mouth as thoughts of the ugly tinseled tree tangled with memories of Derek. What if he didn't show up? Joey didn't need to know about the tree yet.

Two days later, Christmas brought sunlight pouring through a crack in her window blinds, a gleam landing on her closed eyes. Kat rolled over, her arm outstretched, but it landed on the cool sheets of the empty mattress beside her. A dream.

Despite crying for a week, the power of her dream—where Derek held her and told her he was home—would carry her through the day. It had to.

The night before, she'd managed to put the three-foot tree up without vomiting, and all of Joey's gifts were wrapped and underneath it. His fourth Christmas. He almost seemed excited for a giant man dressed in red to break into his house and leave him presents, as long as he didn't have to sit on the man's lap at a mall, party, or store.

In years past, Kat had wanted a picture of her son with Santa. This year, Joey's sanity mattered more. Besides, all of that took energy she didn't have, and they'd had their chance at the monstrous picnic. Why bother now?

It didn't take long for Joey to run into her room and drag her body to the living room. Watching him grin as he opened the gifts helped replace her incessant frown with a slight smile. When his eyes widened at the different rolls of tape, a giggle burst from her lips.

Her gaze fell to the one remaining gift, a framed photo. Derek would definitely come home. He wouldn't miss Christmas.

With most of the gifts opened, Kat hurried and took a shower, something she hadn't done in several days, and picked out a soft red sweater to wear with a silver necklace. Derek always liked the combination. The food waited in the fridge, ready to be heated and served as soon as he arrived.

As Joey pushed a motorcycle around the couch and over her legs, the phone rang. Heartbeats quickened as she yanked the phone from her pocket.

Lisa.

The woman had called several times over the past week. Kat was thankful for her kindness at the hospital, but enough was enough. She silenced the call, wishing Lisa would catch on. Seconds later, the phone rang again.

Ready to silence it, Kat changed her mind after seeing the number.

"Hi, Mom."

"Merry Christmas."

"Merry Christmas."

The line went silent, but Kat decided to wait her mother out.

"So, has Joey had fun?"

"I think so. He's pushing his new motorcycle around the couch."

"And you?"

Kat rolled her eyes. "I'm fine."

"What's Derek up to?"

She hadn't said anything to her parents about her husband leaving. The last time she spoke to them was from the hospital after the scorpion sting. As far as they knew, everything was fine—despite her outrage over Derek's inattentiveness.

"I don't know."

"Isn't he there?"

"No. I haven't seen him since he disappeared last week, but I'm sure he'll come home sometime today."

Silence rolled over the line, and Kat's leg started to bounce.

"Disappeared?"

"Yeah." Kat's chin quivered. "He left a note."

"What did it say?"

"Never mind that, Mom. He's coming back. He just has to come to his senses."

"Kat."

Kat grunted in response.

"What did it say?"

"It said he loves us." She pursed her lips together as shallow breaths overtook her lungs.

"What else?"

"Nothing."

"You've always been a terrible liar."

"I don't want to talk about it."

"So, you've been ignoring it?"

"No. He's coming home."

Her mom scoffed softly.

Kat hung up and slumped further into the couch as the tears took over again.

A half hour later, Joey's first motorcycle broke. She opened another one, and showed him the flashlight.

By afternoon, she dialed Derek's number again. She'd done so every day, at least once.

"Hey, it's Christmas, and we're home waiting for you. Please, Derek, come home. We love you."

As the sun began to set, Kat hugged the wrapped photo to her chest and searched the block for Derek. Was he watching the house from down the street? Why hadn't he come? Tears stung her face, and her vision blurred as she stared at the leaves she'd considered only days before.

Every one still lay whole, unbroken. But she was broken. Wrenching the door open, she dropped the gift to the floor and darted for the leaves. Leaping into the pile and dancing in a circle, her feet crushed each leaf. Tiny pieces caught on her pants and flew into her hair.

Joey appeared at the door, and she led him to the leaves, where he jumped up and down too. Kat shook the tree, and a few more leaves fell to the crushed gravel below. She encouraged Joey. He hopped on top of them, giggling at the satisfying crunch.

She lifted her eyes to the branches. A few leaves still clung to the tree, unwilling to fall. A cast of yellow still colored them. They weren't ready. Well, neither was she.

Derek would come home. No one could tell her differently. If she waited years on end for her husband to return, so be it. That was her choice, and she could make it her reality.

A few weeks passed before a key turned in the lock of Kat's front door, and she stood up from the couch, rushing to greet...

Her mother gathered her in her arms as tears immediately fell from swollen eyes.

"What have you done today?" her mother asked, pulling away from her.

Kat lowered her eyes. "I've been waiting for Derek."

"He's not coming Kat. I know it's hard, but it's time to accept that and make a plan. Your father and I have space at our house."

"No, this is my home. I may not know where my husband is, but he's sending money from somewhere, and I have savings available until he gets back."

"Well, I'm here to get you out of bed in the morning and help you find work. You can't live on savings."

Kat bit her lip, wondering whether to argue or say thank you. Joey kept Kat going. His needs came first and his therapies continued, but other than that, Kat was a raving mess. Finally, she nodded at her mother.

"Great. Go shower before you stink up the whole house, and change your clothes."

Kat winced as she walked down the hall. So far, she'd only told her parents about Derek leaving. The restaurant knew, and Kat had ignored numerous calls from Lisa. Part of her wanted to answer, to talk, but the rest of her wanted nothing more than to hide away like the hermit she'd become. No matter where she walked or what she looked at, everything reminded her of her husband. How had she lost him? Only in moments of sheer honesty would she admit she had, and only to herself. A month. They'd never fought longer than a week. With a month gone, she recognized the lies she told herself. Still, she told them, and she wouldn't stop, not yet.

The shower water relaxed her tense muscles, and she let her tears mix with the streams running down her face and dropping to her chest. Her mama had come. Relief coursed through her as she held onto that one little piece of comfort.

There'd be no babying. That wasn't her mom's way. But her mom loved her, something Derek, evidently, couldn't do any more. No, Derek did love her, her and Joey, and he would come back. *He'll come home. He will.* She curtly nodded as she shut off the shower and swaddled herself in a towel.

"Mom, he's coming back. I know it. He's coming back!" she shouted the words as she clung to the towel rack in her bathroom, tears rolling down her cheeks again.

Survival Kit

The blaring noise brought Kat's fist down with a *whomp*, but it didn't stop. Throwing a pillow over her head she tried to ignore it. It got louder. As she rolled over, she cracked an eye open, and her arm hit the pillow she'd thrown. "Mom, go away."

"Nope. Today you start life over."

Kat rolled away. "I can't start a life over without dying."

"So, your plan is to rot to death in your bed?"

The noise stopped, and the mattress sank behind her from her mother's weight. "I'm not cleaning up that mess. Besides, Joey's waiting for you."

She rolled over and glared at her mother. "You woke him up."

"Darn tootin' I did. Now get up and take care of your son."

"Fine. I'll get up."

The door closed, and Kat growled under her breath, once again feeding herself the same lies she had for a month. Derek would return home. Her mother had no purpose being there. She and Joey were fine. She wasn't depressed.

As the last thought fluttered through her mind, her attempt to ignore reality faltered, and her jelly-like legs collapsed in the closet as tears stroked her cheeks.

How did people do this? She was hardly the only abandoned mother on the planet. Single women lined the grocery store aisles every evening. Whether abandoned or not, they raised children alone. Still, the notion of doing anything without Derek hammered at her head and heart. Then came Joey's suffering. What would happen to him? If she had to work... No, she'd find a way to live off the money Derek sent. Joey needed his mother, not a babysitter.

She brushed the tears away and grabbed her most comfy set of jeans and a T-shirt, her decision made. The only thing standing in her way: Mom. Her shoulders drooped. As an adult, making decisions came naturally with age, except when Kat's mom invaded her home. Tears invaded her eyes again, and she blinked rapidly, hoping to win the battle before she found herself in the kitchen creating toast shapes.

Joey yanked the fridge open as Kat turned the corner. Her mom sat at the table and watched.

"Joey. Close the fridge." Kat rushed over and pushed the door closed.

He fell to the floor, his head knocking on the tile as he screamed. She handed him his cards.

"Are you thirsty?"

The head banging continued. He'd refused the cards she'd made since returning from the hospital. The speech therapist, Emily, thought he might be ready to talk, but he still refused to say anything or use the cards. Kat wondered why so much of the therapists' suggestions seemed like trial and error. A lot of it didn't appear to work. Yet she followed through. Now wasn't the time to choose different methods. She'd talk to Emily next week.

"Are you thirsty?" she repeated. "I'll get you a drink. Say, *I'm thirsty.*"

He knocked his head on the floor again, but this time he eyed Kat and slowed his descent.

"Say, *I'm thirsty,* and you can have a drink. Do you want milk or juice?"

The one-sided conversation continued for several minutes. Kat repeating herself as Joey slowed his head banging. Kat refused to look at her mother. The typical meltdown made everyone's day better. Kat scoffed.

"Joey, I'm not going to stand here all day."

Throwing her hands in the air, she stalked to the table and slumped into a chair. Ear-piercing shrieks split the air.

"That's all. You let him scream?" Kat's mother raised an eyebrow.

"How would you do it, Mom?"

"I'd pour him a drink and tell him that's it."

Kat huffed and shook her head. How had she ever imagined her mother could handle Joey by herself long term?

"Go ahead." Kat waved her limp arm toward Joey.

Her mother's eyes narrowed, and she stepped the few feet to the fridge. Joey watched as she pulled a blue cup from the cabinet. A lucky guess.

"Open the fridge for Grandma, Joey."

Joey opened the fridge.

A smug look crossed Kat's face as her mother placed the cup on the counter instead of in Joey's hands. She did, however, allow Joey to slide the juice partway out of the fridge. An indication of what he wanted.

"Thank you, Joey."

As he reached for the cup, her mother pushed it back on the counter.

"Just a second. Let me pour you some."

With a small amount in the cup, she handed it to Joey. He peered at it and fell to the ground.

"I guess you don't want any then." Grandma pursed her lips and sat down. "Kat what are you doing about this?"

Kat shrugged. "You chose the right cup, and you let him show you the juice. But he holds the cup while you pour, and you have to watch for his nearly-impossible-to-see signal that you've given him the amount he wants."

When the tile no longer glommed onto her feet like the cement floor at a dollar movie theater, Kat helped Joey get the drink he wanted.

"Do you want toast for breakfast?"

When her son didn't growl or throw anything, she placed two slices of bread in the toaster and checked with him about spreads and shapes. The golden-brown toast slathered in peanut butter and cut into half-circles, a new favorite shape, soon slid in front of Joey. One look at the raised eyebrow on her mother's face, and Kat stood up.

"What?" Her mother asked.

"You're asking me what?" Kat's fingers flicked at the thick air like angry star bursts as she inhaled deeply. "You're the one sitting there as if I don't know how to parent my son. If you're here to tell me to stop giving in to him, leave. I cut his toast into shapes, and he learns his shapes. I let him choose what color cup he uses, and he learns his colors. And honestly, I don't care what he eats on his toast!"

"I only wondered how often you're dealing with these tantrums. I thought they were getting better."

Kat closed her eyes and pinched the bridge of her nose. "I'm sorry." Her voice broke as she returned to her seat. "They're meltdowns. And they are getting better, but he still has a lot of them."

"All these therapies, do they help?"

"I think so, but it's slow." She paused and pushed on her bouncing knee. "Mom, I don't know how to do this without Derek."

The chair scratched at the tile floor as her mother moved it closer. With an arm around Kat, she leaned forward. "You will. Not all at once, but you will. Now," she said, standing up and brushing her hands down the sides of her legs, "where're your cleaning supplies. Today we tackle the house, together."

Kat's head landed on the table with a thud.

"I don't want you cleaning my house."

"Great. Get up and do it yourself."

Kat scanned the room. The counter had groceries still in bags from three days ago, and Joey's toys were scattered across the floor of the living room. Pieces of lint collected on the carpet she hadn't vacuumed in over a week. She had managed to sweep yesterday. Thank goodness. Though she had no visual of the bathrooms, she couldn't remember how long it had been since she'd wiped them down, let alone cleaned them.

The greatest desire to throw her hands in the air and put everything off for another day pecked at her mind, and she fell onto the couch face first.

"Kat, get up. We're doing this together. You start with the toys."

Kat's fingernails dug into the cushion, hiding her face and muffling her words. "I can't."

"You can. One toy at a time. Joey can help."

Kat groaned as she slid from the couch to the floor. Every toy and their containers were scattered from wall to wall. Blocks, books, cars, tiny Bricks, giant Bricks. The clutter hid the rug underneath—one still wielding a soda stain she hadn't bothered to wash. At least she'd soaked the sugary sweetness up. That was something, right?

Pushing the containers against the entertainment console, Kat sluggishly tossed toy after toy in their direction as her mom disappeared down the hall toward the bathrooms. Despite her sour expression and defiant attitude, Kat reminded herself to thank her mom.

With the toys picked up, Kat found the energy to put the groceries away. A clean house had meant the world to her until Derek took off, and as her living space became more livable, she wondered how she'd ever let it get so bad. One small chore after another, some of her fog lifted. She and her mom took breaks each time a batch of laundry finished in the drier. Some might not call it a break, but to her, folding laundry felt almost relaxing.

As any other child would, Joey redeposited a few toys on the floor. But Kat limited him to one set at a time, a rule she now had to reteach him due to her lack of consistency over the past month.

Although the anguish in her heart remained, working to bring her house back into order helped neutralize it. For a little while.

Bright hues of tangerine and coral colored the sky to the west. And Kat curled into the corner of the couch, her mom having volunteered to get Joey ready for bed. Recent memories of the day flitted through her mind. The raw emotions that coursed through her earlier had settled into the pit of her stomach—not gone—but better contained. Tomorrow, her mother would have another step for her to take, but she refused to consider what it might be.

The softness of the couch lured her head back, and she closed her eyes. As the couch transformed into a fluffy cloud, the doorbell rang.

Startled, she shuffled to the window and peeked at the unannounced visitor. Lisa, with a basket on her arm and her daughter in tow, waited on the other side of the door. The ignored phone calls had caught up to Kat.

"Hi, Lisa."

Lisa's smile widened. "I'm so glad to see you. I've been worried sick."

"You have no reason to worry about me."

"Of course I do. You're my friend."

Kat grinned, hoping her confusion didn't reach her eyes. She'd appreciated talking to Lisa at the hospital after Joey's scorpion sting, but the word *friends* wasn't the one she'd choose to describe them. Maybe *acquaintances*.

"Kat," her mother called from behind her. "Invite your friends in."

Inwardly scowling, Kat opened the door wider. "Lisa, this is my mom, Edith. Mom, Lisa and her daughter, Bailey."

"I'm so glad you stopped by. I think Kat's mentioned your name once or twice."

Lisa laughed. "I doubt it. We've only talked a handful of times. But I love Kat to death"—she leaned closer to Edith—"even if she does have a habit of ignoring phone calls."

Kat's smile tightened. "Sorry about that. Things around here have been a little crazy."

"That's why I brought you a survival kit."

"A what?"

Lisa placed the basket on the table. "A survival kit. If my husband did to me what yours did to you, I couldn't survive without these items."

Kat raised her eyebrows and shook her head once in her mother's direction, adding a shrug at the last minute.

"Let's see, we have several kinds of chocolate, dark, milk, with nuts, with caramel, and with both. Slippers." She held the slippers up. "Aren't they cute? I love the ladybugs, and the antennas make me laugh." Placing them back in the basket, she listed the rest of the contents. "Tissue, Redbox codes, popcorn, bubble bath—don't worry—I got the good stuff, scented wax with a warmer in case you don't have one, and homemade chocolate chip cookies. Mine are the best."

"You didn't have to do any of this, Lisa. Thank you."

Kat gaped at the basket, immediately thinking of the empty space behind the beans and franks. Tears welled in her eyes.

Lisa waved Kat off. "It's nothing. Now, where's that sweet boy of yours? Bailey has a gift for him too."

"He's in his room rocking," Edith said. "I'll hang out with the kids while you two visit."

Kat attempted to scowl at her mother, but she never looked back.

"Your house is so cozy." Lisa sat on the couch and waited for Kat to do the same. "He's been gone a month?"

"About that." Kat answered. "Do you know if anyone from Baja has heard from him at all?"

"Not a word."

"What about money? I can't believe he left you high and dry like that. You don't work, right?"

Kat shook her head. "His last paycheck was deposited, and then more was deposited a second time from somewhere."

"But not enough to survive on. I don't know what I'd do if I had to figure out how to support myself and Bailey. Her dance lessons alone—" She waved her hand with a quick shake of her head. "Sorry. I'm working on that."

Kat couldn't help but chuckle. "I'm not too worried. I expect he'll show up sometime in the next few days, maybe a week."

A pounding beat against her eardrums as she lied to Lisa and herself, again.

"Do you really think so? I don't know, Kat. It doesn't seem likely, but I've never been in your situation. Has he left like this before?"

She shook her head.

"And you haven't filed?"

"Why would I? I didn't walk away from the marriage." Tension snuck out with the words.

"I know you didn't. And he's on my and Mitch's naughty list for how he's treated you." Lisa bowed her head and studied her fingers. "Do you think he'll file?"

Kat cocked her head. "He said he would, but nothing's shown up."

"Will you let me know if it does?"

Kat stared at the woman, then exhaled sharply. "Why do you care? It's not like we hang out or anything."

Lisa's lips tightened as her posture deteriorated for a split second before recovering. "I'd like to hang out. Don't you like having friends?"

Kat winced. "I'm sorry, Lisa. It's been a really hard month."

Lisa patted Kat's leg. "I know. Now tell me about Joey and his therapies. I want to learn all about you two."

Tension Treatments

The next morning, Kat rolled out of bed on her own and crawled into the shower. As the hot water beat down on her, she wondered what her mother had planned for the day. Sore muscles and stiff joints heightened her concerns. As much as a clean house made mentally functioning easier, her physical movement suffered.

Water cascaded across her back and shoulders, and memories of the previous evening mixed with thoughts of her mom's visit. She wouldn't leave until Kat's life had stitched itself together. She twisted her mouth to the side. It could be worse. Kat could still be despondent on the couch, letting life pile up around her, and would be if her mom weren't there. She sighed. Honesty sucked.

Eventually, her ruminations drifted toward Lisa. The woman never complained. In the past, she'd bragged about her daughter nonstop, but last night she stopped and apologized. As Kat rinsed her hair, she found herself wondering about the cost of Bailey's dance lessons. Lisa had probably intended to share that amount before catching herself. They couldn't be cheap. And the friend thing? The woman had always talked to Kat at business events, but friends? Did she want to be friends with a woman who lived perfection?

After pushing the water from her eyes, she grabbed a towel and tried to focus on the day. Without her mother there, she and Joey would eat and pick up. The spotless house needed little of that. Then the bus would come for Joey, and she'd go grocery shopping. But they hadn't used the food from her last trip. When Joey got home, they'd play until OT started. Her knee bounced. She could handle a day of Joey at school and a little work for herself, but Mom? No way—she'd have something planned. With a groan, Kat ambled into the kitchen.

"Oh good, you're up."

"Morning, Mom."

"Joey has certain activities today, right? School? That kind of thing?"

"Yes." She reached into the fridge for the milk and snatched a banana off the counter.

Her mother eyed her. "That's not a breakfast."

"It is today." Kat bit into the banana.

"Joey's schedule. Quick, you don't have much time."

Kat glared at her mother. "What are you talking about? I have all day."

"You have an hour."

Kat's jaw dropped.

"Don't stare at me like that, Kat. You need a day to relax."

"I relax at home just fine."

With one arm on her hip, her mom forced a pencil into Kat's hand. "His schedule."

"Mom, I'm not going anywhere."

"The appointment's set. A day at the spa. You can enjoy it or spend your day worrying for nothing, but you're not staying home."

"No."

Her mother's hands gripped her shoulders and moved her toward the hall.

"You think you're the only one capable of taking care of Joey. Well, you're not."

"I know that." Kat turned around and folded her arms.

"Do you? When was the last time you left him with someone?"

"He goes to school twice a week."

Her mother narrowed her eyes. "School doesn't count."

"The last time I left him with someone else, he ended up with stitches."

"From an injury he could have gotten with you. Get ready. You're leaving."

Fire pricked at the edges of Kat's eyes. "I can't, Mom."

"You can. And today you're going to realize it." Her mom's hand rubbed down her arm to her hand. "It's me. I raised you, and you turned out okay."

"He's different."

"And I'll learn. Get ready."

Wanting to stomp her feet like a little girl, Kat traipsed into her room and closed the door. Where did her mother get off telling her what to do? That right ended the day she turned eighteen. Well, the day she got married. Apparently, it started again a month after her husband abandoned her. She yanked her hair into a tight ponytail and slammed her feet into some flip flops. It's not like looking good mattered at a spa. Holding up her hand, she watched as it shook in front of her. The tight feeling in her chest caused shallow breaths, and a sudden dizziness came over her. She flopped onto her bed and curled into a ball.

She couldn't leave Joey. She just couldn't. He was her life line, the only thing helping her through Derek's crap. Returning to daily activities—okay—but not more than that. Leaving Joey meant leaving behind the only part of Derek she still had. Sobs fell, muffled by the pillow.

A soft knock at the door sounded, and she sat up, wiping at her eyes. "I'm not leaving."

Her mom peeked into the room before entering with a soft smile and sat next to her. "Tell me your plans for living without Derek and his income."

"He's sent me money. He'll send more."

"He has to support himself too, Kat."

"He's coming back, Mom!" She leaped from the bed with tightened fists, the yells burning her throat. "He's coming back! He loves us. Autism sucks. It's hard, and he needed a break, but he won't abandon us. He won't abandon me!"

Her chest lifted and fell in a harsh rhythm as she scowled at her mother with tight lips and flared nostrils. Silence engulfed them, and her mother looked down at her own hands.

Tears coursed down Kat's face again. This time she let them fall. Down her neck. Onto her chest. To the floor. None of her muscles moved.

Arms soon ensconced her, and she thought to fling them away, but instead melted into them, a little girl with her mama.

"I can't do this, Mom. Not without Derek. How am I supposed to move on when I love him so much?"

"One step at a time. Joey needs you. He needs you to let him grow as much as he needs you to give him hugs. All moms suffer separation anxiety. It doesn't matter if the kid's got autism or not. We worry about every one of their firsts. We stand with our arms outstretched when they take their first steps. There's more than you even know.

"Your dad had to tie my hands to keep me from calling you every day when you left for college and again when you got married."

She rubbed at Kat's arms as she continued. "But moms have to let go, and you have more responsibilities to that boy now that Derek's gone, for however long it may be. So let's start small. I'm taking care of him today. Grandma. I love him as much as I love you. Trust me and give me your phone. If I need you, I'll call the spa."

Kat sniffed. "My phone?"

"Yes. You have to put it in a locker anyway." She handed her a book with a printed page sticking out of it. "Take this. The address and services you'll receive are on the paper. It's a great book. I read it last week."

Kat eyed it. "Fantasy?"

"You think I'm going to hand you anything with romance as the main plot? Not in your state of mind." She winked at Kat.

As they walked out of the room, Joey shuffled sleepily across the hall and into Kat's arms.

"Good morning," she whispered as she picked him up and hugged him tight.

He laid his head on her shoulder.

"Joey, Mama has to leave, but Grandma will be with you. She'll make you breakfast and lunch and even help get you on the school bus, okay?"

The question went unanswered, as she expected it to.

"I love you." She kissed his head and placed him on the couch. A faint gratitude rooted in her heart. "Thanks, Mom."

The front door shut behind her, and she tried to stroll to the car. If she had to spend the day at the spa, she might as well try to enjoy it.

Kat held the printed information in her hand and gawked at the hand-scrawled information. Not only had her mother booked her at one of the nicest spas in town, she'd paid for three treatments and a lunch. The exorbitant gift knotted her stomach. Though able to afford most of their wants and needs, her parents' budget still required they watch their nickels and dimes. The amount spent on Kat for a single day deprived them of one of their weekend getaways. One person, one day, for the price of a weekend for two. Superfluous. Kat scratched her brow and slid out of her car.

Palm trees lined the spa's parking lot and paths as vibrant flowers in pinks and purples, reds and yellows perfumed the air, hiding the desert rock underneath. Fountains adorned the outer entrance, their azure tiles mimicking the blue of the distant ocean.

Kat took a deep breath. Mom had Joey. She could do this.

Immediately greeted, Kat soon found herself wrapped in a luxurious robe and led to what they called the relaxation room. Large windows overlooked a lake, while overstuffed leather chairs with footstools welcomed guests waiting for sessions. As she scooted into the offered leather chair, an attendant placed a cup of fruit-infused water on the end table next to her.

"Your first session begins in ten minutes."

Kat nodded and eased the water cup to her lips, the light essences of lemon and cranberry sweeping across her taste buds. Her eyes scanned the room. Digital pictures from the state's most exotic locations decorated the walls. Other, smaller walls, held shelves of geodes, minerals, and precious stones. But none of them held a single clock. Unconsciously stroking her wrist, nightmares of what her mother and Joey might be facing surfaced. She'd never thrown away those shoes that bothered his feet, and she hadn't walked her mom through how to prepare his toast. And lunch.

What would they do for lunch? The shudder of her heart and pressure in her throat forced her mouth open, and she gasped for air. Was it possible to forget to breathe?

Seizing her cup of water, she downed it all in three large swallows. The mantra of her day began. *I'm here to relax. Try to relax. I'm here to relax...*

A short time later, an attendant led her into a private room.

"You have three treatments and a picnic lunch scheduled today. We'd like to start with your body treatment. Is this your first time at a spa?"

"No. But I've never had a body treatment." Kat bit her lip as she clutched the side of her robe.

"You'll love it. Like a massage, a sheet covers you everywhere, except where we are working. Go ahead and lie down on the table under the top sheet. I'll be back once you're ready."

When the therapist returned, she explained the process for the detoxifying wrap Kat's mother had ordered. This time, Kat closed her eyes and allowed the aromatherapy to enliven her senses and lure her into a peaceful place as she reminded herself that Joey was at school.

Sore muscles, tightened from housework and obvious stresses, struggled to relax during the following massage, but as Kat continued with her mantra, her body lightened, and she longed for the feeling of weightlessness to continue.

The rest of her day consisted of a lunch by the private lake and a facial. By the time everything had finished, she happily lounged in the relaxation room for the suggested hour. Thoughts of Joey and her mom still pecked their way into her mind, but since no one had summoned her to an emergency phone call, she supposed their happiness mirrored her own. She refused to consider the meltdowns she assumed her mom and Leah had dealt with through the afternoon.

Sooner than she hoped, a touch on her shoulder let her know the hour had passed.

On the way home, each muscle praised her mother. The spa had stripped months of tension and stress away, even from her skin and, somehow, her mind. If only such pampering happened monthly. Daily?

As the car came to a stop in the driveway, Kat faced the tree in the front yard. The last of the leaves had finally fallen to the ground. Exiting the car, she stepped over to the pile and chose two perfect leaves, then entered the house. Her mother soon peeked around the corner from the kitchen, and Kat hurried over, wrapping her arms around her.

"Thank you, Mama!"

"Mama, huh? It must have been good."

"It was. None of my muscle sting, pull, or ache. My skin is super soft... I don't know why I fought—"

The ringing bell brought Kat's head around, and she furrowed her brow as she padded toward the door.

"Kathryn Burns?" The man stood with a clipboard and the city-required lanyard.

"Yes?"

"I have a delivery. Please sign here."

"Do you know what it is, or what company it's from? I'm not expecting anything."

"No Ma'am." He held out a manila envelope.

Taking it in her hand, she closed the door, her hands shaking.

"What is it?" her mom asked.

"I don't know."

Unlatching the top, Kat reached into the package and retrieved the pile of papers inside.

Every bit of tension returned, and once again, she forgot to breathe.

Petition Party

Without thought, her feet transported her forward. Staring at the words on the front page she willed them to change. Instead, they blurred as drop after draining drop fell from her eyes. Anger thrust itself into her heart, trying to replace anguish with each threatening heartbeat. Rude names and crass words lit her tongue, stinging as they exited her mouth. As she entered her room, the packet landed on the bed, and two perfect brown leaves fluttered to the floor. She scowled at them, then smashed one with her heel, the brash crackle popping in her ears. Her foot raised high into the air again and froze before fury dropped it next to the other leaf. Leaving it there, she plummeted to the floor, her fists striking the wall behind.

The gaze of her wild eyes tore across the room and fell to the phone she'd left home at her mom's request.

Ripping it from the charger, she punched in Derek's number. The recorded message stated his number was no longer in service, and she launched the device across the room, watching it hit the opposite wall and tumble to the floor.

"Kat?"

"I'm fine. Leave me alone."

"Dinner's in ten."

"I don't care about dinner!"

Sobs rippled through her body, every muscle aching as she processed the delivery. Divorce papers. It was real. He'd left for good.

Time passed slowly, and the room darkened around her. Lights emanating from various electronics reflected red and green against the otherwise unseen walls. She stared, unfocused, at the surroundings. Her whimpers long-ago quieted, she crawled to her phone and flipped through the contacts. Numbers of friends she hadn't spoken to since Joey's birth splayed across the screen. She imagined the call. *Hi, I haven't talked to you in four years. My husband abandoned me. Make me feel better, please.*

Tacky.

Tears threatened again.

Another swipe of her contacts list, and her finger hovered over Lisa's profile.

Kat counted the rings.

"Hello?"

Kat's chin quivered as her voice caught in her throat.

"Hello? Kat?"

"Yeah." The word squeaked past her lips.

"Oh, Kat. I'm sorry."

Blubbering from Kat's mouth echoed in her ears, but it wouldn't clear. Kat gasped. "Y-you knew?"

"Suspected is probably a better word." Lisa paused then asked, "They came today?"

"Y-yeah."

"Did you read through them or rip them into shreds?"

Kat snorted. "I threw them on my bed and flung myself against a wall to cry for three hours in the dark."

"Make a copy tomorrow because we're having a divorce document burning party."

Kat's head fell into her hand. "A what?"

"A divorce document burning party. These aren't the ones you sign, right?"

"I don't know," Kat said, flatly.

"You're still sitting in the dark, aren't you?"

"How'd you—"

"Just a guess."

Kat could almost hear Lisa smiling sadly through the phone.

"It's time to turn the light on." Lisa continued. "We're going to look at them together."

Kat's eyes narrowed as she got to her feet. "Look at them on the phone?"

"I'll listen."

The light flicked on, and Kat blinked as her eyes adjusted to the change. Climbing onto the bed, she gathered the pile of thrown papers, shuffling them to align the strays.

"I've got them."

"First things first, what are they exactly?"

"A Petition for Divorce."

"That sounds more like asking for the dissolution of marriage than papers you sign to make the divorce final. Don't you think?"

Kat exhaled sharply. "I guess so."

"Didn't you tell me last night that he left you everything and said he'd send money?"

"Yeah."

"Find the page stating what you get. So help me, if he doesn't list enough money for you, I'll hire your lawyer."

"No you won't." Kat's response sounded sharper than she intended. "I'm sure he listed a high enough amount."

"He abandoned you, Kat."

Her eyes burned again. She blinked quickly, forcing her emotions back.

"Found it. The house and all the contents. My car. Full custody. Of course, because he's hated Joey since his diagnosis—"

"Really?"

"I don't know. It seems like it. Who doesn't want to see their own son?"

Lisa growled.

"And..." Kat's eyes widened. "The alimony and child support is fair."

"Are you sure? Don't limit yourself."

"Right now, I want nothing more than to stomp on his head, but the money's fair."

"How fair, Kat?" Lisa's tone reeked of disbelief.

"Mortgage, utilities, and gasoline-for-a-month fair. He must be living on nothing."

"Or found himself a fantastic job."

Kat dropped the forms on the bed again. "Where though, Lisa? I have no idea where he is. Shouldn't I know that?"

The line quieted and the burning built into tears that no amount of blinking could curb.

"Yes," Lisa said. "They don't list an address?"

"A P.O. box."

"Never mind that. He stopped being decent when he walked away from his wife and son."

"But he is decent. He worked hard and gave the best hugs. He loved us. And this money..."

"Kat, you need the money. He's giving it to you because he knows it. But if he loved you enough, he wouldn't have left."

"Maybe."

"Definitely. So, where are you going to make copies tomorrow? Because come evening, you, Joey, and your mom are coming here to burn some nasty papers, eat burgers—or whatever Joey eats—and roast marshmallows."

"Chicken nuggets, but I prefer burgers. And I have no idea."

"The UPS Store if you have to. Six o'clock sharp tomorrow. I'll text you my address."

Kat didn't know whether to laugh or cry, but the faint giggle that escaped felt good.

Curling into the blankets on the bed, she rolled away from the papers. A moment later, she received a text and smiled.

"Joey, get your shoes." Kat gathered the copies she'd made at the library.

"He's not listening."

Kat rolled her eyes. "Thanks, Mom."

Her mom's plan of getting Kat back to normal, included Kat continuing to do most things for her son. Had she thought about it, she would have made sure his shoes were on before gathering the papers. She put her purse and the paperwork on the table then chased after Joey. When she caught him, she held his waist and knelt down.

"Joey, where are your shoes?"

He glanced at the closet.

"Please get them, so we can go."

A look from under hooded brows accompanied pouty lips.

"Let's get them together."

Gently tugging on his hand, she led him to the closet and asked him to pick up his shoes. This time he obeyed.

"Thank you. Do you want to put them on now or in the car?"

His tiny feet rushed his body to the door, where he waited for someone to open it.

Kat's mom folded her arms. "You're letting him go barefoot?"

"For now."

"Hope his toes don't fall off from the cold." The muttered words reached their intended target.

"The seventy-two degree weather brings a lot of frostbite, but I'm willing to risk it through the seconds it takes him to reach the car."

Her mother's chest raised, followed by the corners of her mouth, as she forced a cough. "You're going to get through all of this just fine."

Kat groaned as she opened the door. "Let's not dwell too much on what I have to get through."

"You're going to have to deal with it at some point."

"I know, Mom. And I appreciate your help, but tonight I don't want to talk about finding work or figuring out childcare. I want to burn some papers, scream at Derek, and come home to bed. Can we do that?"

Her mother's arms slipped around her shoulder as they walked to the car. "That sounds like a great idea."

The roller coaster ride of emotions her mother provided that day had Kat ready to disappear herself. One second she demanded Kat log all of Joey's schedule, needs, and triggers, as if that were possible, and the next she told her to take a break and read for a bit. Everywhere Kat looked, she found job listings, ranging from convenience store cashiers to nail techs, taped to a wall. Never mind that one position often ended up being robbed at gunpoint, and the other required training Kat didn't have.

The idea of childcare bothered Kat the most. Yes, her mother cared for Joey for a full day with basic success. Nothing broke and they were both alive. But finding someone trustworthy and willing to watch him full-time? It wasn't going to happen. Not even Mandie garnered that much trust. In between all the compliments, Kat's mom showered her with reality. Words telling her to change splattered the sentences intended to make her feel better.

Thankfully, the car ride to Lisa's remained quiet. Most of the time.

"Look at this neighborhood." Kat's mother gawked at the large houses set back into larger lots. "Did you know Lisa lived in a place like this?"

The house, only a couple of miles from Kat's, rested in a county island surrounded by tract homes. Each two-acre lot held a large ranch-style home. As Kat turned onto Lisa's property, she noticed the lack of seventies flare shared by the other homes on the block. No one could accuse her of lacking style.

"I had an idea. Her daughter attends the same school Joey will."

"Is that so? And her husband works for Baja Burgers like Derek did?"

"Yeah, but in the corporate office, Senior Vice President or something like that."

"You always did know how to pick friends."

Kat bit her lip. If she and Lisa were friends, why were her hands sweaty and her legs threatening to bounce? The phone conversation helped calm her down, and she liked the notion of burning the divorce petition, but friends? A visit at the hospital and a basket full of feel-betters followed by a *call me when the papers come* coalesced like ingredients in a cake. Charity. Asking about Joey, listening to her woes, all of it boiled down to nothing more than an on-going service project. Yet Kat lapped it up. Her stomach twisted.

"Let's go home." The whispered words lingered in the car as she met her mom's eyes.

"Why?"

She pursed her lips and studied the ceiling of the car. "Because I don't want charity."

"Charity or not, you need to get in there. This woman deserves a thank you at the very least. You can't cancel last minute."

"I'll say I'm sick."

"And she'd rush dinner right over."

Kat sighed as she climbed out of the vehicle. "I know. Let's go."

Lisa opened the oversized door with a flourish. "Come in. I'm so glad you came. Bailey's been talking about it all day. Even at her ballet rehearsal. They've been working on Swan Lake."

"How wonderful." Kat forced the words out.

No matter what Kat tried, she couldn't help but scan the large living space. The beautiful pine ceiling with wrought iron decor, accenting leather furniture, and solid, rustic wood tables, consoles, and buffets welcomed them into the home. Kat gazed at the walls where large photos of red rock slot canyons hung above each couch. Paintings of the Grand Canyon and Canyon de Chelly adorned the walls of the attached dining room.

"I thought we'd sit outside. Mitch has a fire started, and the weather is so nice," Lisa said.

"Sounds lovely." Kat gave her mother a sideways glance, prompting her to speak.

"How long have you lived here?" Edith asked.

"About six months. We lived in the East Valley, but Mitch wanted to live closer to the office."

"Your home is beautiful." Edith raised her brows at Kat, who ignored her fascination with the larger home.

"Thank you. We've done a lot, but there's so much more to do."

"Well," Kat said, "You'd never know it."

Kat herded Joey out the door and relaxed at the sight of a large play area with swings. Allowing Joey to pull on her arm, she followed. "Do you mind if he plays on the toys?"

"Not at all." Lisa grinned. "Bailey would love to help him."

She called Bailey over, and Kat smiled weakly.

"I don't know. He's finicky about who helps him."

"I'll go." Edith patted Kat's shoulder. "Looks like there's a perfect spot for me to sit and watch them."

"Thanks Edith," Lisa said. "I'll send a drink over for you. What would you like?"

"Coke if you have one."

"We do." Lisa waved the kids away and led Kat nearer to the fire, inviting her to sit in an Adirondack chair. Once seated, she motioned to Mitch who hurried to get Edith's drink delivered.

"That's awfully nice of him," Kat said, after turning down a drink.

"He wants to make sure we have a good time tonight." Lisa grinned as her gaze followed her husband. "Mitch built these chairs and has done a lot of the work around here himself."

"How does he find the time?"

"He either decides to make it a family activity, or he works at night with floodlights. Sometimes Bailey and I work with him under the lights. The experience isn't necessarily fun, but I always enjoy the results."

"I can see why."

"Have you had a chance to look through those pages a little more?"

Kat sighed. "Yeah. If I want to speed things up by a few days, I can sign the uncontested paperwork, then everything's done in sixty days."

"That's great, if it's what you want."

"I haven't really decided. Part of me wants to make him sweat it out, waiting for everything to go through. The rest of me? Blech." She threw her arms in the air. "I wish I could burn the real set."

"I have a whole planned event for the copies. We'll do it after dinner."

Kat smiled, then stole a glance at the kids playing on the slides.

"It's nice that your mom came. Where is she from?" Lisa asked.

Kat settled back in the seat and met her eyes. "Queen Creek."

"That's not too far; close enough for day trips."

"Yeah. You'd think so."

Lisa chuckled.

"I love my mom, but she literally came to push me back into the world."

"And you're not ready."

"It's not getting back in the world that's hard. It's leaving Joey with someone else. I'm a stay-at-home mom. That's my job."

Lisa nodded. "It was. Not anymore."

Kat glared at her. What right did Lisa have to weigh in on the subject?

"I'm sorry, it's probably not my place to say anything, but you're going to have to leave Joey with someone else eventually. What happens when you start dating again?"

The guffaw that rumbled past Kat's lips brought heat into her cheeks. "I'm never dating again."

"I bet you do."

Kat worked to reign in her pettiness, but it poured out anyway. "You hardly know me."

Lisa raised an eyebrow. "I guess not, but I keep trying."

Turning her head, Kat stared at the open sky. "I don't understand why. Am I a charity case or something? We've talked a few times at corporate events, then when Joey got stung, you suddenly decided we should be friends? I don't get it."

The dim lights kept her from seeing Lisa's face, but the soft sniffing told her enough. The woman was crying. Kat bowed her head, begging her heart to slow and her obviously misplaced anger to simmer.

"I'm sorry, Lisa. That came out all wrong. But I look at you and all you have... Our situations are so different. And then you show up and are so wonderful during the hardest time of my life. I haven't had a friend in a long time, and I feel like a charity case because you're so nice."

Sobbing giggles burst out of Lisa. "You don't want to be my friend because I'm nice?"

Kat tightened her lips, trying not to laugh, and finally managed to say, "No. I don't want to be a charity case."

Lisa settled further down into her chair. "In my mind, I'm literally begging you to be my friend. I have a lot of stuff, but I don't have that."

"Do you bribe all your friends?" Kat giggled as she met Lisa's gaze pointedly.

"That's what I mean. What friends?"

The flat question rang in Kat's ears. "I'm rusty at the whole friendship thing myself. Tell you what, how about you stop giving me baskets full of wonderful gifts, and I recognize how we are becoming friends."

"No gifts?"

Kat rolled her eyes. "Maybe an occasional candy bar and a twenty dollar limit on Christmas and birthday gifts."

"I can do that." Lisa lifted her head. "Are we becoming friends?"

Memories of her dark room and flicking through the contacts on her phone floated to the forefront of Kat's mind. "You're the only one I thought to call last night. We're friends."

It didn't take long before the aroma of grilling beef, seasoned with all the right spices, soon wafted through the air. Lisa suggested they gather the children and clean them up for dinner.

"It takes some time for Joey to transition," Kat said as they walked toward the playground. "I need to give him some warnings, especially when he's having so much fun."

"Show me how it's done."

Kat enjoyed the feel of the winter grass trailing across the sides of her sandaled feet and turned to Lisa. "Does Mitch take care of your lawn too?"

"Oh no. We have a landscaper for that." She held up her thumbs. "Brown thumbs. Both of us."

"Me too."

Stopping at the edge of the sand, Kat called Joey until he looked at her, and then gave him a five-minute warning, hoping it would be enough. At three minutes, she started calling out every sixty seconds. At thirty seconds, he crawled to the highest point of the play structure, showing no intention of coming down.

Kat pointed. "This is a transition fail."

After slipping off her sandals, she stepped to the structure and worked to convince Joey to slide down the big slide. Another fail. As she climbed the structure herself, she continued to talk to him about dinner and marshmallows and other activities. He turned away from her. Her approach ended, and she squatted next to him.

"Don't you want chicken nuggets?"

He shook his head. Kat cringed.

"How about you and me and Bailey eat up here?"

"And me!" Lisa called.

"Grandma might want to come up too. Do you think there's room?" Kat asked Joey.

He nodded, his eyes brightening.

"Great." Kat's gaze fell on her mother. "Will you bring up some wipes to clean our hands?"

"Sure will," Edith said.

"Stay here, Joey. I'll get your food." Kat patted Joey's head before climbing down.

The sounds of laughter during dinner brought a peace to Kat's heart she'd almost forgotten. Bailey talked to Joey, accepting his lack of answers. The young girl beamed and pointed at the stars and moon. Once in a while, he viewed them with her. Lisa and Kat enjoyed a lighter conversation with her mom. Kat missed the easy conversation that came with friends, and she found herself wondering if she could find it again with Lisa.

After everyone had finished eating, Lisa stood, brushing the dust off her pants.

"The fire is almost burned down to perfect glowing coals and ready for marshmallows, but first, we have to have a little ceremony."

Kat took the dishes down, while her mom helped Joey, who luckily wanted to roast marshmallows. At the fire pit, Lisa stood on a chair with her arms spread. "Edith, watch the kids, you never know what might explode when it comes to a dying marriage."

Kat's mom shook her head, a grin crossing her face, as she helped the kids sit together in a single chair away from the fire.

The divorce petition crinkled in the breeze as Kat clutched it, ready to add flame to the fire. But Lisa stopped her.

"How many pages are there?"

Thumbing through them, Kat quickly counted. "Fifteen."

"Really? Okay, I'm ready." Lisa shook out her hands. "Today we gather to scorch the divorce petition served to Kathryn Burns by the man she once loved. With the first page, we shed tears for that which is lost."

Kat tossed in a page. The flame soon sparkled blue and green, and she raised her eyes to Lisa in wonder.

"The next four burn with a welcomed goodbye." Lisa flicked her hand toward the fire, motioning to Kat.

The pages fluttered into the coals and bright green and blues again joined the flickering flames as they burst from underneath, brightening Kat's solemn visage.

"With the passing of this life, a new one begins." Lisa held up five fingers.

As the pages found their way into the soft coals, flames rose in purples and pinks.

"We celebrate climbing new mountains and soaring above old experiences. We celebrate a new beginning filled with twists and turns, wonderment and love. We celebrate Kat."

Colors burst toward the sky, burning through the last of the pages and lighting the faces of the participants and audience. Joey and Bailey's faces split into grins as they bounced next to Edith. Soft explosions of green and blue continued, followed by pinks and purples. The warmth on Kat's hands as they covered her mouth and nose went almost unnoticed as she watched the flames dance in the fire pit. Lisa dropped her arms and head, and the last of the colors disappeared, the soft glow of the coals returning.

A single tear glistened under Kat's eye as she gazed at the fire pit, a smile on her face. Lisa patted her shoulder, and Kat dragged her into a hug. "Thank you."

Napkin Notes

The next night, Kat glowered at the computer screen as she searched for late evening and night jobs. If she had to work, she'd rather miss Joey's sleeping hours. Lists of janitorial jobs, convenience store clerks, and skilled jobs covered the screen. Copies of her stark-white resume littered her desk, proving she lacked the necessary training required for the well-paying positions. Some college and an old part-time job as a high school graduate made her point fairly well: *I have no education and no experience; hire me at your own risk.*

The thud that followed her head flopping against the desk, rattled in her ears. How did other women do this? Leave their children and enter the workforce? Kat understood that many women chose to work, but she wasn't choosing to.

After talking to Mandie, Kat felt a little better about leaving Joey in the evenings and at night. She still didn't like it. But Mandie agreed to extend her hours and record respite hours after therapy until Kat returned.

Technically, respite hours weren't supposed to be used for childcare. The state intended parents to use them for date nights and as time for themselves. Still, Kat had read too many horror stories of daycare providers and abuses. Then came the challenge of finding night care. She refused to consider anything else. She'd spend the mornings and most of the day with Joey. Period. As long as Joey had respite hours, she'd use Mandie. Hopefully, he wouldn't run out, and the state wouldn't question the heavy increase of usage. She supposed divorce, alone, was explanation enough.

Lifting her head, Kat made a list of a few open positions that didn't make her quite as nauseous. Mail sorter, a motel night clerk, and a customer-service rep at a call center. Would eleven to fifteen dollars an hour even make a difference? With Derek sending as much as he was, she considered using savings and waiting until Joey started school.

The door squeaked, and she turned to meet her mom's eyes.

"How's the search?"

"Awful. I think I'll wait. Live off savings for a couple of years and try for something else when Joey starts school."

Her mom sighed. "Well, it's better than trying to live off the money from Derek for the rest of your life, but no."

"Why not? I have several thousand left. I can make it last."

"And when your car breaks down or you get sick? What if you're in an accident? Stop being ridiculous."

Kat tossed her head back and stared at the ceiling. "I'm trying. Mandie's agreed to come in the evening and stay super late, but I'm not ready."

"Why are you doing that to Mandie?"

"Doing what? She gets paid as well as I will."

Her mom sat on the desk. "She deserves a life outside of this house."

Flames burned through Kat's chest and into her extremities. "And I don't?"

"Of course you do, but—"

"Mom. If I have to work, someone has to watch Joey. It's the whole reason I don't want to work. Do you think I'm being lazy?"

"Not at—"

"Don't you think Joey deserves the best care he can receive without me around?"

"Yes, but—"

"Well, it can't be me if I'm working, and it can't be you unless you move closer. Doesn't Dad miss you, anyway?"

"Stop yelling at me, Kat." A warm red flowed across her mother's face.

Kat folded her arms and huffed.

"I shouldn't have said that." Her mom bowed her head. "I know you mean the best for Joey, but Mandie's young."

"She's not much younger than me." Kat shoved her hand down her leg and clutched her shaking thigh.

"Maybe not."

"But you really think that, don't you? That her taking care of Joey at night takes advantage of her, whereas me working outside of the home has no impact."

Her mom's eyebrows raised. "No impact? It definitely has an impact. On both you and Joey. But I'm not certain it's a bad one."

"Oh, so the impact it makes on Mandie is a bad one?"

"Will you drop that? It doesn't affect her differently, except that she's single and lives with roommates, and I assume she dates on occasion."

Kat shook her head. Because she'd been married, technically still was, and lived with her son instead of roommates, she had to work and Mandie shouldn't? Asinine.

"You're not making sense, Mom!" Her hands flew in the air as the words left her mouth.

She lunged for the door, but her mom stepped to the side, blocking it.

"I screwed up when I said that. I'm sorry. The difference is you're in crisis mode, which requires living differently for a short period of time, and Mandie isn't."

Tears swam in the bottoms of her eyelids as she glared at her mom. Sinking to the floor, she hid her face. Crisis mode. What did that mean for her? Every waking minute of every night and day spent taking care of everyone and everything but herself? When hadn't she done that? In the past year, her entire life had fallen apart. The second she decided to seek help for Joey, her life stopped. Crisis took over. Each breath plummeted her deeper into despair, and it wasn't just the last few hours, days or weeks, but since Joey's diagnosis. Just as she started to understand autism, her marriage disintegrated in front of her. Crisis one morphed into crisis two. Or were they the same crisis?

"I can't do crisis mode anymore." She cried into her fists and wiped at her nose as snot ran toward her hand. "I don't want to. I need time to think, to understand my own thoughts. I can't remember the last time I had a full day for that. Why can't I have that?" She flung her arms out. "Everyone else gets to consider themselves!"

Her mom's blurry face appeared next to hers. "You'll have it again. And the sooner you find a job, the sooner you can get to that point. Pick yourself up, and let's start applying for some of these.

"Not now."

"Kat, you can't put them off forever like this."

"I'm not. But I am putting it off for today."

She pushed past her mom and slid into her shoes before leaving the house.

The car's engine revved to life, and she backed into the street. Emotions stabbed at her heart as she blinked to clear her eyes. Flashes of light struck the windshield and rearview mirror. Traffic noise pounded in her ears. She turned the stereo up, then immediately turned it off. Coming to a stop at a red light, her open palms hit the steering wheel several times, as her countenance broke into ragged pieces that morphed into an unrecognizable mask.

As the light turned green, Kat removed herself from the road, coming to a stop in the dimly-lit lot of a worn strip mall.

Allowing all of her emotions to course through her, she accepted the pain and loss, frustration and anxiety. Begrudgingly, she recognized the happiness she found in Joey and the love given to her by her mother and Lisa. A little more time, and she admitted the love she had for them. With a little encouragement from her more reasonable side, she rummaged through her purse until a pen and scraps of paper bulged from her fist.

A list of expenses was soon scrawled across one torn receipt, and various math problems covered the back of another. Biting her lip, she rested her head in her palm against the driver's side window. Living off savings and funds from Derek required her to scrimp for more than a year. No incidentals. No new clothing for her. No going out for dinner or eating more than rice and beans. None of it surprised her, but she had to see it written out. Her mom was right. She had to accept her new life.

As she scanned the storefront signs, her stomach growled. The process of acceptance needed to continue, but not at home.

Climbing out of the car, she shuffled to the small pizza parlor located in the line of stores.

The cold water doused with spritzes of fresh lemon eased the last of the pain in Kat's throat, and she took another bite of pizza. Several napkins covered in various notes, math, and names littered the table in front of her. The grumbles in her belly, long subsided, were replaced with the pleasing effect of comfort food. Emotions, still close to the surface, no longer stabbed at her heart. The strength she'd lost months before trickled into her veins. It was time.

With a tip placed under the empty pizza pan, Kat stuffed the inked napkins in her purse and hurried outside. The brisk air rushed against her skin. A sweater would have been nice. As she slipped into her seat, she pushed air through her rounded lips and started the engine.

Once home, she padded her way to the computer, careful not to wake Joey and her mom. Her fingernails clicked at the keys as she attempted to rework her feeble resume. Stay-at-home moms went back to work all the time. Somehow, they made themselves look good enough to be hired. She didn't expect a job requiring specialized skills, but she had what it took to land a job requiring good personal and professional skills. Google helped locate appropriate phrasing: detail-oriented, efficient budgeter, active researcher, interpersonal skills.

She'd picked three feasible jobs earlier in the evening and filled out those applications first. Next came the few she hoped wouldn't cause her stomach to roil too violently. Then, with a groan and a yawn, she finished two applications for day jobs. Her research at the pizza parlor proved day jobs weren't in her best interest. Not only would she be away from Joey, but Mandie couldn't watch Joey during the day, which increased Kat's expenses. However, day jobs did put more food on the table than trying to live off savings.

Rising to her feet, Kat shuffled out of the room. Her mom stood against the opposite wall with folded arms.

"Glad you made it home."

"Sorry." Kat winced. "I shouldn't have left Joey with you like that."

Her mom rolled her eyes. Kat almost laughed, recognizing where she'd picked up the habit.

"I'm not concerned about Joey," her mom said, "but you can't go running off like that."

"Mom, I'm sorry." She took a step toward her bedroom. "You're probably right, and I'm done arguing tonight."

"Were you able to work things out?"

The words, softer than before, caught Kat's attention.

"For now."

"Good."

In her room, Kat leaned against the wall and peered at her bathroom, vision fuzzing as her mind blanked. Stress, though somewhat lessened, tightened her muscles, while exhaustion slapped at her mind. The combustible combination kept her from climbing into bed. A slow blink brought her eyes to the bottle of bubble bath from Lisa's gift basket.

Water soon flowed into the soaking tub, silky bubbles floating on top. With her phone on the charger, she played soft music through a speaker. Then, with a single brown leaf in her hand, she sank her toes into the warm water. A quiet moan formed in her throat, and tension eased from muscles as she lowered herself below the soapy surface.

The Beginning

"Have you heard anything?"

Lisa's question went unanswered as Kat's thoughts flowed freely for a time. They lounged near the play area in Lisa's yard, watching the kids play, and peace warmed her heart as Joey smiled at Bailey. He used to never smile at other children.

Eventually, she reminisced about job applications as she prepared to answer Lisa. Several weeks had passed since applying for the first few jobs, and she hadn't stopped. Though, she still contemplated each position carefully, unwilling to apply for just anything.

"I have a couple of interviews set up, but nothing I'm super hyped about," Kat finally answered.

"Are you super hyped about any job?" Lisa laughed as she knocked her shoulder into Kat's.

Cool granules of sand fell from the tops of Kat's feet as she shifted. "How do you keep the cats out of here?"

Lisa eyed her with a lowered chin and a raised brow.

Kat pressed her lips together and closed her eyes, taking a big breath. "I don't know. None of the work is earth shattering, and I go back and forth. Would I like working as a motel clerk during the height of check-in? Do you think they enforce smiling?"

Lisa shrugged with a soft giggle. "I'm sure it's preferred."

"In that case, I might prefer the bank call center. They pay better anyway. Besides, I can sound like I'm smiling without actually smiling. See?"

"That was...great."

They each started laughing, and Kat stole a glance at Joey.

"I don't want to leave him."

"What are you planning to do when he starts full-time school in a year? He's almost four, right?"

"Next month." Kat shook her head. "I don't know. Work at the school?"

"It's not a bad idea, but don't you think he'll do better if you learn to leave him with other people on occasion?"

"Sure, make it about him." Kat shoulders dropped as she scoffed.

"Poor thing, you didn't even make it to the kindergarten cry." Lisa patted her back.

"I know. And I was really looking forward to losing it then instead of now."

The breeze brushed through Kat's hair, a few pieces flitting into her eyes. Pushing them behind her ear, she glanced at Lisa.

"What's it like staying home when Bailey's gone all day? How do you handle it?"

Lisa leaned back in her chair, her eyes scanning the sky.

"I'm bored. Conversation with myself lacks a certain quality."

"Another person?"

"Yeah." Lisa grinned and dropped her gaze to Kat's. "I've actually considered applying for a few jobs myself. Something at a school is perfect. I'd have the same schedule as Bailey and could still handle all of her activities while being around people. There's an opening at the middle school."

"For what?"

"A receptionist."

Kat wrinkled her nose and Lisa laughed.

"I don't mind smiling at people," Lisa said.

"Think of all the angry parents."

"I'll send them to the principal. Not my problem."

Kat reached for her drink, sipping at the fresh-squeezed lemonade.

"Something tells me it doesn't work that way."

"Probably not." Lisa patted the sand over her feet with her hand. "Hey, Bailey's dance recital is Saturday at two. She's worked so hard, and I can't believe the growth she's made. Her teacher says she's a real natural. Will you come? Mitch'll be out of town."

"I don't think Joey would do well sitting in a chair with music, clapping, and a crowd."

Lisa scrunched her nose, a glint shining in her eyes. "Call it practice."

"Practice..."

"You have to leave him sometime. When's your mom leaving, anyway?"

"Not soon enough." She rubbed her hands along the side of her pants. "I love her, and she's been so much help, but living with her as an adult is getting a bit old."

Old might not have been the best word choice, but it was the kindest. Kat's mother helped tremendously, but she also needled Kat about every little thing. Her choices mattered as long as they matched her mom's. Now that Kat recognized what she had to do, her mother's help seemed more like an interference.

"I've always wondered what living with my parents again would be like. Never seemed right," Lisa said.

"They wanted me to move in with them."

"Ouch."

"Yeah. Anyway, I think she's planning to leave Friday, which means she couldn't watch Joey Saturday." Kat shrugged almost apologetically.

By Friday afternoon, Kat curled onto the guest room bed with tears in her eyes. Two job interviews, neither from jobs she wanted, and the flat look in both interviewers' eyes screamed disinterest. Now her mom's packed suitcase sat on the floor, while she lay in the fetal position, rocking similarly to her son. She'd be alone. What had made her think her mom's leaving would make things better? Just watching her pack sent waves of anxiety through Kat's heart.

"You'll be fine."

Kat raised her eyes to her mother's, but said nothing.

"You'll get other interviews, and eventually someone will offer you a position."

She attempted to nod, but the heaviness of her head stopped most of the movement.

"Mandie loves Joey, and she already prepares his meals and bathes him."

"But, I want to put him to bed." The words pushed past her lips, stinging her tongue on the way out. "It's my job to do that."

"You can take a day job."

"No. Even financially, a late shift makes the most sense, especially with Joey's respite hours."

"Are you sure that's how you want to work things?"

"I don't want to work anything, remember?" Kat sighed. "I'm sure. A lot of single women do it this way."

Her mom snorted.

"When you think about the tax dollars, Mom, think about Joey. He's your money at work."

"Helps some."

The room filled with a thick silence again, and Kat's mom slipped onto the bed next to her. Her arm draped over Kat, whose head rested on a pillow. Kat curled closer.

"I can't do this," Kat whispered.

"You can. You already are."

Kat scoffed.

"When I got here, your house looked like a war zone. You and Joey both had on dirty clothes, and you stank."

"I did not!"

"You did! It was terrible. Why do you think I sent you to shower so quickly?"

Kat rolled her eyes, but a soft smile raised the tips of her mouth.

"Now you're getting up on your own and are back to being you. Mostly. You're healing, and that's good. Give it more time. Just don't pedal backward."

"That would be bad." Kat choked on the truthfulness of the words.

Her mom got to her feet and tugged on Kat's arm until she stood next to her. Rubbing her hands down Kat's arms, her eyes glistened. "You're amazing. I don't think anyone could handle such a situation better than you have. Derek left without warning. You had no time to consider the implications or how you would care for yourself and Joey in such circumstances. But now you know."

Kat tried to smile, but her face fell.

"Yeah. Wish I liked it."

"You can't have everything you want."

The suitcase lifted from the floor.

"Dad wants me to miss rush hour. I'm already late."

"I'm sure he'll be happy to have you home."

"He could have come to visit."

"Dad? Drive here on his own?" Kat giggled.

"It's not like it's far."

"No, but he knew I needed my mama." She threw her arms around her mom. "Thank you."

A short hand squeeze later, and her mom sat in the car, waiting for Kat to move so the door could close. "I'm not far."

"I know."

"You're not alone."

Kat smiled and swung the car door closed and then waved as her mom drove away.

The knock at the door made Kat jump even though she expected it. Squeezing and releasing her fist once, she stepped over to answer it, her purse hanging from her shoulder.

"Hi, Mandie."

Mandie grinned. "Are you ready for this?"

Kat grabbed her stomach with one arm. "No."

"It'll get easier," Mandie said as she walked inside. "Any leads on work?"

"I have an interview on Monday with a call center that offers night hours."

"Great. I'm ready when you are."

"Yeah. I'm not sure that'll happen."

"Sure it will, and you need breaks like today for yourself."

"Maybe, but I don't know that a six-year-old's dance recital counts as time for me." She laughed nervously.

"It's a start." Mandie chuckled.

Kat looked back at Joey. Dropping her purse, she rushed to him and coaxed his eyes to hers as she crouched down.

His hair shifted as she combed her fingers through it before kissing the top of his head. "Mandie's here if you need her. You be good, and I'll be back in a little bit."

She blinked back tears.

"I can do this." The mumbled words were for her, but she gazed at Mandie and repeated it louder. "I can do this."

"Yes you can."

Despite the warming air outside, shivers ran down her arms as she slid into the driver's seat. Taking shallow breaths, she started the engine. Two hours. Three hours max. Then she'd be home. She could do this. She had to do this. The car rolled down the driveway and into the street.

The short drive to the rented elementary multi-purpose room barely gave Kat enough time to gather her thoughts, let alone relax her breathing.

Her hand sat on the door handle for several seconds before she dropped it to her lap. Which cartoon was it that said something about courage wasn't the same as being fearless? She didn't remember, but she hoped it was right.

Taking two deep breaths first, she pushed the car door open and slid one foot to the pavement. Another breath, and she twisted in the seat, bringing her other leg out. A fourth, and she rose to her feet and took a step, followed by another.

What kind of an idiot buckled under the pressure of leaving their child with his therapist? Mandie loved Joey. More importantly, Joey loved Mandie. The small pieces of growth they'd seen had come largely in part because of the work Mandie did with him.

The soles of her shoes tapped on the sidewalk as she stepped up from the asphalt. Maybe her mom had a point. Joey did need to be around other people. But he was. Wasn't he? He spent time at school and with Bailey. Her shoulders dropped. It didn't change the truth. She had to work. She had to. And Joey would have to stay with someone else.

A few stray strands of hair ruffled at the top of her head as she walked under the blowers at the double doors. Lisa waved her arm straight in the air as she perched in a half-sitting position over her chair. Kat swallowed deeply and flicked her fingers at her friend. As she reached her seat, Lisa bumped her shoulder.

"I'm so glad you came. How are your nerves?"

Kat met her eyes. "I'm a baby."

Lisa chuckled. "It'll get easier."

Phone in hand and set to vibrate, Kat stared at the screen.

"Oh no." Lisa shook her head. "You are not going to stare at that screen with my precious daughter on stage."

"But if something happens—"

"Then you'll feel it vibrate in your pocket."

Stuffing the phone in her back pocket, Kat narrowed her eyes at Lisa. "You planned this with my mom, didn't you?"

"Didn't even talk to her, but I should have."

Kat snorted.

The lights dimmed, and Lisa grabbed Kat's arm, hugging it to herself. "After this, we're bringing ice cream to your house to celebrate."

"Of course you are." Kat chuckled, and her heart began to slow as she worked to pay attention to the stage.

A woman with red hair knelt at the edge of the platform near the stairs. An irritated splotch, where she bit her lip, now traveled toward her chin. As the woman waited with tension in her shoulders, little girls in pink tutus scuttled across the stage. One with bright red curls stopped near the curtain, tears in her eyes and fingers near her tiny set of lips that someone had painted crimson. The woman switched to a crouching position and tried to shoo the girl back to the line the others had formed. Instead, the girl's little feet, covered in soft ballet slippers, darted down the stairs at the side of the stage, her tutu crumpling as she fell into the woman's arms.

What a darling girl. Too bad her mother couldn't see her dance.

Kat shifted uncomfortably in her chair. She didn't know the girl, her parents, or their situation, but she could guess. Some kids suffered separation anxiety. She tightened the grip on her leg. The likelihood of Joey performing on stage seemed minuscule, yet he'd never shown symptoms of anxiety when climbing on the bus or entering his classroom. And when a three-year-old girl dressed in a tutu cries from stage fright, it's cute. A grown man hovering at his mother's knee isn't.

Besides, she wanted Joey to learn independence. Dreams of him attaining a decent job with good pay had not once been dashed. It's why she pushed therapies and researched and tried to understand autism as much as she did. Because he deserved to grow up and have everything, conceivable or not. After all, no one could say what a three-year-old would become twenty years later. Not doctors, not teachers, not parents. Advancements were made every day.

But Joey craved consistency. He didn't just crave it. He needed it. If she hovered, keeping him to herself when he wasn't at school, wouldn't it make it harder for him later? Everyone, literally everyone, kept telling her it would. Why hadn't she listened?

She wouldn't work if she had a choice. Dreams of staying home and raising children had never changed either. If Joey didn't have autism, she probably would have brushed off the stitches. An empty pit formed in her stomach at the idea of Derek being right. Still, Mandie accomplished much more than Nancy, and the benefits of the change outweighed everything else. Derek could have half-credit, at best... A surge of roiling blood coursed through her veins as she reconsidered and quickly deemed the abandonment of his family worthy of no credit.

Bailey's group padded onto the stage in leotards and flowing tissue-hemmed skirts. A smile erupted over Lisa's face, and Kat couldn't help but smile herself. Each girl stood with their feet together and arms curved above their heads. Bailey grinned bigger than all the others.

How often did Lisa leave Bailey with sitters? The question crossed Kat's mind, and she struggled to not ask right then. That girl, grinning on stage, held her mother's heart in her hand. Lisa gave her everything, especially attention.

When the recital ended, Kat waited for Lisa and Bailey. Thrumming heartbeats struck her ribcage. She ignored them and smiled as Lisa hugged Bailey and handed her a large bouquet of roses. A light chuckle formed in Kat's throat, but she choked it back down. How long would those last?

Mother and daughter circled the room a couple of times, and Kat considered leaving, but refused. A few extra minutes promised to help her accomplish her new goal: let Joey grow.

Twenty minutes passed before Kat drove home where Lisa and Bailey joined her at the front door with a bucket of ice cream. The pounding in Kat's chest had quieted some, and she wondered when it would stop completely. After walking Mandie to the door and overwhelming her with thanks, Kat pulled Joey into her arms and gave him a hug until he pushed her away and returned to his motorcycle. Bailey picked up a broken one to push around the couch behind him, willing to play side by side.

As her friend scooped ice cream into the large waffle cones and plastic bowls, Kat leaned across the counter. "How often did Bailey stay with a sitter before she started school?"

"Mitch and I try to have a date night once a week."

"And you pull it off?" Kat's eyes opened wide as the words spurted from her tongue.

Lisa laughed. "Not every week. Stuff comes up."

The crease in Kat's brow deepened. "When did you start?"

"As soon as she took a bottle."

"Ouch."

"Not *ouch*. Important. I would have killed Mitch without that time away. He needed it too, even though he'd never admit it."

Kat bowed her head and studied her fingers.

"Bailey, Joey, come have some ice cream." Lisa scooted two bowls of ice cream across the table.

Joey sat down, looked at the bowl and spoon with the waffle cone on top and started eating.

Lisa grinned at Kat and nodded. "I'm getting better at knowing what he'll eat. No cherries."

Kat narrowed her eyes. "When have you given him ice cream?"

"Never. But you told me about the ice cream disaster at the restaurant when we had our barbecue."

"I did?"

"Yup. Apparently, it wasn't important enough to make the history books though." Lisa paused, and glanced at her. "How'd you do tonight?"

Kat closed her eyes and tightened her lips as she regarded the question.

"I've decided I'd rather be you than a mother who stands at the stage waiting for her child to maybe fall apart."

Lisa handed her a bowl of ice cream, and they each sat next to their child.

It didn't take long before Lisa called Bailey from Joey's room and headed out the door. Walking into the late-afternoon light with them, the pavement warming her feet, Kat's heart brimmed with a peace she hadn't expected.

"You know," she said, "I'm glad I practiced today."

"I like having company. Next month's is on the twenty-third."

"Once a month?"

Lisa chuckled at Kat's failed attempt to hide a groan. "Yup. But Mitch is supposed to come."

"Hopefully, I'll be working."

"Monday, right?"

Kat nodded.

Moments later, she watched as Lisa's car disappeared down the street. Raising her head, she gazed at the bright sky, glad for the beautiful spring weather that came early in the desert. Reminded of the day before, the words her mother spoke entered her mind. *You're not alone.* Lowering her eyes, she caught a glimpse of the tree in her front yard. Small green shoots replaced the leaves that had shed several weeks before. New and tender, each clung to the branch in groups, one supported by another.

Smiling, she ran into the house and to Joey's room where he rocked in his chair. Little arms clutched hers as she picked him up and sat down in the rocker with him sitting on her lap, facing her.

"Hi! Have we met?"

Joey nodded.

"Well, what's your name."

A twinkle shone in his eyes.

"I know, your name is Samuel."

He shook his head.

"No? Then it must be Jack."

He giggled, shaking his head harder.

"No? I know what your name is. You're David!"

"I not David. I Joey!"

"You're Joey! That's right." She tightened her arms around him, his head resting on her shoulder as his little hands played with the supple sleeves of her T-shirt. With an invigorating breath, she reveled in the soft scent of her beautiful boy.

"I sure do love you, Joey."

About I Not David

The story of *I Not David* grasped me as I contemplated what kind of story I might have within me. I wasn't surprised; after all, my second son has autism.

The behaviors he showed at a young age helped shape this fictional story. In fact, his hand was crushed in a step stool. I rushed from of another room to a shriek of painful terror just in time to watch him rip his fingers out from between the bars. He also carried around a fan to keep him from electrocuting himself, and he learned to remove his bedroom door from the hinges much earlier than I anticipated.

Many of the heart-wrenching emotions Kat experiences come from my memories of learning what autism is and how to deal with the professionals assigned to help me. It took some time, and every once in a while, we run into something I haven't quite figured out. Luckily, my husband supports me through it all. He has listened to me fall apart after IEP meetings as well as long days, usually during the little bit of time we've scraped together for ourselves. For the record, I am less succinct when speaking.

Having a child with autism, though, has taught me more than it has hindered me. I see the world a little differently now. My son taught me to celebrate the little victories and let the unimportant nothings go by the wayside. My day brightens when he lays his seventeen-year-old head in my lap hoping for a back rub. And his knowledge of computers means I have someone to help me when my husband isn't home and my computer screen turns pink while I'm writing. When I'm sick, he's the first one to take care of me. The days that I'm away, he's the only one I trust to cook dinner.

So, while autism can be scary at first, those who have it are absolutely wonderful. I always tell the professionals that I wouldn't change my son for anything in the world, but I would take away the things that make his life harder.

Isn't that how parents everywhere feel? Maybe. Well, we can leave a few hard things so that our children can grow, but no more than that.

Free Download

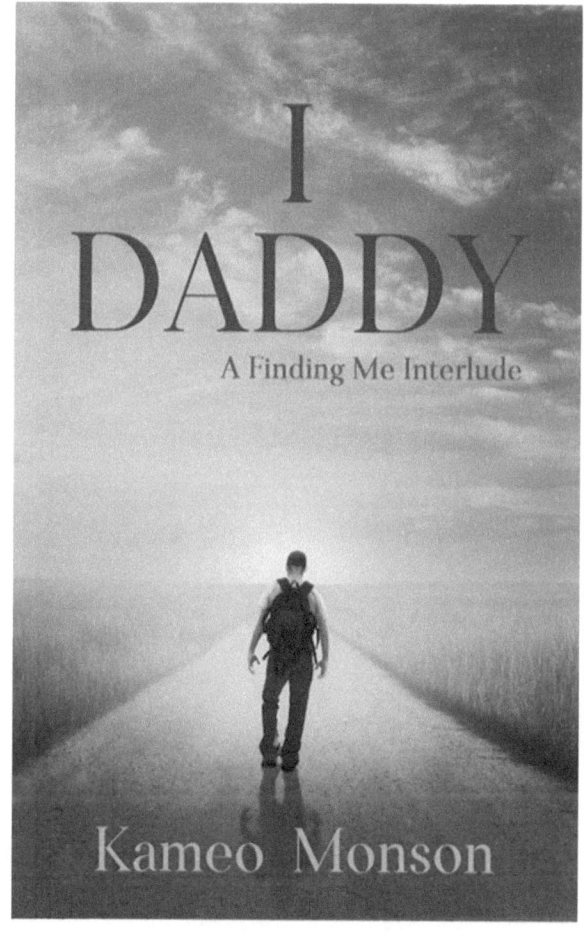

What happens to Derek?
Find out in the full-length novel
I Daddy: A Finding Me Interlude

Download for free at KameoMonson.com

About the Author

Kameo Monson, a mother to four teenagers, began her writing career as a review blogger. Since then, she has written two novels with plenty more to come. A lover of all kinds of literature, Kameo has found her niche in women's fiction, where she often focuses on love and family.

Other hobbies include music, spending time with her family, petting her dogs, rats, Guinea pig, or cat, and enjoying the fresh air of the Arizona mountains.

As a native Sonoran Desert dweller, she hopes to one day be a reverse snowbird and plans to take her loving husband along for the ride.

Stay connected:

Follow me on Facebook: @KMonson.author
Follow me on Twitter: @KameoMonson
Sign-up for my newsletter at KameoMonson.com
Email me at KMonson.author@gmail.com

Acknowledgments

Many people have helped me as I've prepared this book. Once again, I'm grateful to my husband who supports me in every way, including my writing and publishing dreams. My children have handled my disappearance into obscurity with love and understanding. I might sit in the same room, but my mind is often in another world. My sister, a wonderful nurse, has helped me with certain medical questions. I'd probably get something wrong without her. Thank you to all of my family.

Members of the Flinch-Free Fiction and LDS Beta Readers groups on Facebook have helped me keep my sanity as I've written and rewritten passages. They've also provided me with the bulk of my beta readers. Thank you for keeping me from cracking.

Misty McKenzie and Kristal Coles both spend more time than they probably want to listening to me talk about writing and publishing. I'm lucky to have them as friends.

Lara with Wynter Designs has created another beautiful cover for me. She always does beautiful work. Thank you.

Craig D. Barton spent many hours editing and proofreading *I NOT David*, and he has agreed to continue working through the rest of the *Finding Me* series. I couldn't publish without some like him behind me. His skills are top-notch.

And, thank you to my readers. Without you, these words would disappear into the black hole of unread books.

Now Available

In digital (Amazon only) and paperback formats.

Coming soon:

I Not Buddy: Finding Me Book Two